Once Upon a Wolf

TIEGAN CLYNE
SCARLETT SNOW

COPYRIGHT

This is a work of fiction. Any resemblance of characters to actual persons, living, dead, or undead, events, places or names is purely coincidental. No part of this book may be reproduced or transferred in any form or by any means, without the written permission of the authors. Uploading and distribution of this book via the Internet or via any other means without a permission of the authors is illegal and punishable by law.

Text copyright © 2019 Tiegan Clyne & Scarlett Snow

All Rights Reserved

Map and formatting by Zoe Perdita @ Rainbow Danger Designs: https://www.facebook.com/groups/420088805183447/

Editing by Fresh Eyes Editing: https://www.facebook.com/groups/738786986523437

Cover design by Christian Bentulan: http://coversbychristian.com

With special thanks to beta readers: Mandi Ladd, Jordan Simpson, Desiree Hayman, Margaret Ball, and Elyssa Davis. Thank you so much!

For all the bad ass witches who fight for their own happily ever afters.

Rebecca,

All my love,

Scarlett Snow

xx

PREFACE

This book features scenes where some of the characters use American Sign Language (ASL), which is a distinct language that has its own syntax and isn't just another way to speak English. Words and their modifiers can be expressed with hands but also body language, intensity of movement, and facial expressions. However, for the ease of reading and clarity reasons, ASL sentences will be translated into English and shown in ::....::

All telepathic communication between characters and their familiars will also be shown in —...—

CHAPTER ONE

RAVYN

The deeper I venture into the forest, the darker the shadows become. They cling to the trees and reach out with spectral fingers; the darkness at their core responds to the darkness within me. Every other time I've had this feeling, it was welcome. Empowering, even. Tonight the darkness is a reminder of the enormity of the step I'm about to take and it doesn't feel as good.

Up ahead, in a clearing where nothing ever grows, is the Devil's Altar, the place where my coven practices our dark magic. We're the strongest coven in Clan She'ol. The blood of a hundred sacrifices has saturated the ground with the power of our Dark Lord. I've spilled my share of sacrificial blood over the years, with no regrets. Until recently, dark magic has served me well.

There are two academies in the Great Forest: Nevermore, where all the so-called villains go, and Everafter, where the do-gooders gather. Nevermore Academy encourages evil, extreme free-will and general naughtiness, with no promise of a happy ending. Actually, happy endings are something that the students at Nevermore are almost guaranteed to be denied. I guess it comes without saying since the academy is nestled deep in the woods of Draoich, the dark half of the Great Forest.

Everafter Academy, on the other hand, is named for its promise that all of its graduates will find their Happily Ever After. It's one of the most elite schools of the six kingdoms, and so far, it's kept its promise to its students.

My twin sister, Redera, is a witch like me - sort of. She worships the Storyteller, the God of Light, while I worship the Prince of Darkness, Lucifer Morningstar. She's the first white witch to be born in my family for over a hundred years. Naturally, because of her rarity, Everafter made her an offer nobody in their right mind would refuse: four years of the best magical education money could buy, but she wouldn't have to pay a cent, and a guaranteed happy ending. They offered her a full-ride scholarship to a place where "your dreams are only the beginning." That's what her letter said when it wrapped in a gold ribbon that cost more than all of our clothes put together.

I got a letter from Everafter, too. They said they would have made the same offer to me, but unfortunately they have a very strict rule against enrolling students who worship the Prince of Darkness. They don't want my kind corrupting the innocent minds of Fantasia and feel that I'm more suited for Nevermore Academy. Isn't that nice of them to say that?

Sounds like discrimination to me.

I'm officially labeled a villain before I've even committed a crime.

I shouldn't be surprised. Witches aren't exactly welcome anywhere in the Great Forest. Our covens are scattered throughout the kingdoms, but we're mostly in hiding. There are Witch Hunters everywhere, just aching for the chance to hang us or burn us at the stake. Sometimes the covens just hide. Sometimes, the covens fight back and hunt the hunters.

Good times.

Redera isn't just my twin. She's my best friend. The thought of being separated for four whole years is unthinkable. Even though she's a white witch and I'm a dark one, we've always done everything together. We're yin and yang, darkness and light split into two bodies that share the same soul. We've never been apart. If she's going to Everafter, there is no way I'm going to Nevermore.

That's why I'm heading to the clearing at Witching Hour to tell my Dark Lord that I'm switching teams.

I've never actually seen him before. I've felt him when we've had our rituals, and I certainly know the dark presence of his magic in my blood. I've felt his power. The magic I have is granted by him directly through the Church of Shadows and I know might end up losing it when I tell him my plans. His teachings are all about free will, though, so I can't imagine he'd get *too* pissed off when I exercise what he's told us all along is ours to use. Right?

I'm eighteen now. This is my life, my choice. Period.

I reach the stone circle that demarcates the clearing from the forest around it. I pull my red ritual cloak in tight, and lifting my head, I step into the unhallowed space. The air inside the grassless open area is a good ten degrees colder than the air in the trees. I feel the chill all the way to my bones. My long dark hair had been swaying in the breeze, but it stops the instant my feet touch the clearing. Here, there is no wind. I can almost hear the spirits in this place holding their breath, waiting, wondering what I'm about to do.

I walk up to the altar set in the middle of the circle. The stone hums and vibrates from all the power my coven has soaked it with over the years. It's an audible sound, just barely noticeable but definitely there. It shifts in pitch as soon as I put my hands on the cold surface.

"I, Ravyn Hemlock of Clan She'ol, Mandrake Coven, come here of my own free will," I intone, hoping I'm doing this right. Abandoning my religion isn't exactly something Grandma prepared me for. "I have decided for myself how I will live my life. I'm not worshipping the Darkness anymore. From this day onward, I renounce you, Lucifer and all your works. I will worship the God of Light, starting now, from this moment. I no longer serve you."

Something whispers among the trees, a faint hiss that permeates the air.

I keep my palms glued to the surface, but I instinctively look around me, my eyes darting to every possible corner. Dead leaves rustle through the clearing. Branches sway and crack. The hissing grows louder, deeper, *closer*!

An enormous, shadowy creature slithers through the underbrush and my blood freezes in my veins. The hissing is joined by the roaring buzz of a million flies flapping their wings. They pour into the clearing, dive-bombing me *en masse*.

I release the altar and scramble back, my hands and legs trembling in their sockets. *Okay. I get it. The big guy is pissed. Time to go now.*

Watching the flies circling in front of me, I add hastily, "I'm eternally grateful for everything you have given me, my lord, but I want to choose my own path now. I want to be with my sister."

"The path you have *sssselected* is wrong," a deep, disembodied voice whispers. It's so close a rush of hot air brushes my ear.

Fear grabs hold of me. I turn around and run in the direction I came, but the flies cover my hair, my dress, and every inch of my skin. I scream and swat at them, but the more bugs I catch, the more return. All I can do is cover my face with my hands and muffle my screams.

A low chuckle echoes through my mind.

It's *him*.

I can feel his presence in my bones, consuming my mind, body and soul.

I am in deep trouble.

The flies release me and the air returns to my lungs. I remove my trembling hands and watch the insects materialize into a towering shadow. My breath hitches in my throat as I look up at him.

The Fallen One.

The Prince of Lies.

My Unholy Master.

The shadow swirls, revealing a human-like figure. He's bipedal, like a man, but with enormous black bat wings and curling black horns. His face is long and his glowing eyes burn into me like molten lava. He can see through to my soul and the evil in his presence penetrates me to the core, leaving me singed in its wake.

Every hair on my body stands on end as the dark energy radiating from his being seeps into my own. The ground trembles and the trees around me shiver in the Dark Lord's presence. He takes one step toward me. Flames spring up as his cloven hoof strikes the earth, making the soil burn. Tiny fires light dead vegetation with each step. He walks in flames that cause my hair to bristle with static.

I feel like I should prostrate myself before him, but I'm too afraid to move. "F-forgive me, my lord," I stammer pathetically, "but I *need* to be with my twin."

Lucifer chuckles, the sound dark and ominous. "You *need?*"

The shadows gather around him again and he becomes one with the darkness. When he reappears, he's changed and I want to hit my knees in front of him for an entirely different reason. He's still tall, with long, dark curls and the most intense golden eyes I've ever seen. He looks human, but he's so much more than human now. He's angelic. His cheekbones are high and his lips sensual, but cruel. His golden robe is impeccable, but from what I can see, the body beneath it is beyond compare.

Lucifer's angelic form is truly breathtaking. My knees go watery and desire floods through me, consuming every sensation in my body. What the heaven is going on? It's like I'm under a spell that he's cast on me. I've never wanted to fuck anybody more than I want to fuck him right now. I guess this is why mortals say temptation is the devil.

He lifts the corner of his lips into a sinister grin. "Are you *sure* you wish to leave me, child?"

I clear my throat, trying to keep from throwing myself at him. It's a hard fight against every instinct telling me to get down on my knees and worship my Dark Lord like there's no tomorrow. I wonder how he'd feel against my tongue and I wish I could find out. Does he really carry the Inferno's Kiss? Can he really pull out my soul just from one touch of his perfect lips?

"I...I admit you're quite the opposite of what I imagined, my lord, but yes, I'm sure. Positive, really. One hundred percent."

His smile fades and a dark shadow flits over his face, darkening his eyes. "And you are aware of the consequences of rescinding your allegiance?"

I'm not really sure what he means. His tenets have always encouraged us to seek our own paths, to not obey rules we wish to break and to never, ever bow to those we should command. The rule 'do as thou wilt' is the entirety of his law.

"I... I don't know, my lord."

Now I feel so fucking stupid.

Lucifer steps towards me, reaching out one perfectly made masculine hand. His fingertip grazes my cheek, the touch gentle and arousing. I shiver, but this time it's not from fear.

"The consequences of leaving me are these," he whispers, stepping closer so I can feel his body heat, which is considerable. I look up into his glowing eyes and find that I cannot look away. "You will lose your ability to use magic. You will no longer be under my protection. And you..."

He leans closer, his lips brushing against my forehead, making my third eye explode with colors and sensations. I nearly cum on the spot, my body overcome with bursts of electricity. He tugs his lips into a derisive grin.

"You will be nothing more than an ordinary, thankless, defenceless mortal. Nobody will want you. Not even Everafter will take you in."

"But I—"

A hundred images flash within his gaze. I see me and him, entwined on this very altar stone; my twin, walking through the gates of Everafter Academy and closing them behind herself, locking me out; my three-times great-grandmother Esmeralda sacrificing a wolf and another wolf attacking her from behind. I see power and sex and blood and pain. I'm dizzy with the shifting images and visions, but I know what these are.

These are lies.

I find the strength to tell him: "I'll take that chance, my lord."

The smile leaves his face, replaced by a cruel sneer. His eyes turn as black as unlit coals. "Then have your wish, ungrateful wretch!"

Lucifer slams his mouth into mine, the impact painful. My teeth cut into my lips, and he still pushes harder. Without my telling it to, my jaw springs open, and he shoves his tongue deep into my mouth. Orgasm washes through me, and I nearly fall, but he grabs my arms and holds me as I quake and cry out.

Then I feel it.

He's pulling my magic out from me.

The energy rinses out of my soul, leaving just a fading cloud that he devours greedily. I can feel myself deflating, my spirit tearing to surrender the power that came from him. My soul is being shredded; my cry of ecstasy turns into screams of pain, strangled by his mouth still smashed against mine.

It seems to last forever, as if time has no meaning here at the altar. Only Lucifer and I exist, entwined, with his grip on my shoulders strong whilst my body weakens bit by bit.

Finally, he releases me and I fall to the ground in a whimpering heap. Wiping his mouth with the back of his hand, he glares down his nose at me. He's shining, and I remember that when he was an angel, they called him the Dawnbringer.

"You have your wish," he spits callously. "You will live to regret this choice."

I can't speak. All I can do is cry. He transforms back into black smoke, then dissolves into flies that swarm around me before they streak back into the forest and disappear.

Chapter Two

Ravyn

It takes me forever to get home. Without magic, I have no sense of direction and get lost in the woods repeatedly. My frustration is beginning to turn into anger. I'm exhausted and sore, and the latter isn't the good kind. How will I get home? I'm just a mortal now. I can only hope I'll get back before Grandma wakes up at dawn to feed the chickens.

Fucking chickens.

Imagine our surprise when, just last week, Redera adopted a whole coop of them and never planned on using their blood to ward off evil spirits. She just wanted to keep them as pets. Typical Redera. They do produce delicious eggs, though.

I stare down at the moss-covered ground and laugh. Hysteria is threatening to consume me from the sheer exhaustion of this journey. I really never prepared myself for any of this. I never thought about taking Broin's horse for transport, and I had no idea what the consequences would be. I'm still not sure that this is all that Lucifer had threatened me with, and I just want to get home. At least he said his protection will only be lifted from me and my family will remain safe. Safe or not, Grandma will still have a heart attack when she finds out what I've done.

Hopefully, before that happens, she'll remember the Dark Lord's first and foremost Unholy Commandment: *Thou shalt follow no path but thine own.* Obviously he wasn't very pleased that I chose to follow his adversary's path, but still, his Twelve Satanic Tenets and Ten Unholy Commandments said nothing about leaving the Church of Shadows being forbidden, or what punishments there might be if we tried. He taught us to make the most of our lives. To be strong, self-indulgent and to embrace the seven deadly sins. Isn't that what I'm doing?

I *want* to attend Everafter Academy so I can be with my twin and have a better life. Everafter would never accept a Darkblood witch into their school. Renouncing my worship to the Dark Lord was the only way for me to get in. Surely Grandma will understand that? First, though, I've got to get home and face her.

A cool breeze whistles through the trees and lifts my hair as I gaze up at the moon-dappled leaves. The Great Forest is protected by ancient magic that conceals us from the mortal world. Everything inside is like a magical maze that is damn near impossible to navigate unless you have magic. The six kingdoms have made sure of that.

How long have I been here? It feels like forever.

The longer I walk through the forest, the more my exhaustion deepens and plays with my mind. Every step I take is laden with a growing certainty that my footsteps are being followed. It's like a spider that you only see moving from the corner of your eye. My surroundings aren't exactly helping to settle my unease.

Enormous trees twist and tower over me, creating a dense canopy that curtains the sky. But ribbons of moonlight claw through the leaves and cast eerie shadows on the floor. I feel like an insect that's about to be trapped and pulled into a huge web. I've never gotten lost like this before. But I'm a human now and the paths all look the same. With every wrong turn my anger bubbles up to the surface; by the time I do finally reach Hemlock Cottage, I'm spitting mad.

Weariness tugs at my body, making my limbs tremble as I step onto the cobbled path. How do mortals manage to do things when they grow so tired, so easily?

At the end of the path, the lights in our two-story home are turned off and the chimney is smoke-free. I don't think I've ever seen that. The cottage was built in the late seventeenth century and contains many of the original furnishings. It's pleasant in summer but dreadful in winter, which is why Grandma always has a fire on. As for the lights, Redera is afraid of the dark, so our bedroom light is *always* switched on at dusk.

A feeling of ice-cold dread creeps over my shoulders.

I hold my breath and take another step, raising my fists just in case.

Someone grabs me from behind and spins me around. My hand goes down through a hidden slit in my skirt to the sheath strapped to my thigh. I come up with my dagger. The enchantment that should have made my hands tingle is missing, probably sucked dry by Lucifer, but the edge is still sharp. I press that edge of the blade into the throat of the man who grabbed me.

"*It's me*," Broin shouts in a whisper.

Broin Blackstone, a long-time friend of the family and my Daddy, puts his hand over my mouth and his arm around my waist. His crimson eyes are wide with fear, but I know that he's not afraid of me. Broin isn't afraid of anything. I frown up at him, all fight gone in the face of his obvious alarm. He shakes his head sharply and seizes my dagger hand in an almost painful grip.

"Hurry," he whispers, pulling me back into the woods.

He's got the instincts of a druid, born from years as a hunter, and he leads me quickly through the brambles and underbrush. He can pass without a single branch grabbing at him, but I'm not so lucky. Apparently when Lucifer made me unmagical, he also made me clumsy. I crash through the vegetation after him; Broin gives me a hard look, probably wondering what's wrong with me. I just shrug helplessly and follow where he leads. He's never appeared this alarmed before. Something is clearly amiss, but questions will have to come later.

He takes me to his cabin nestled among the trees. Once we're inside, he activates the wards Grandma gave him to repay him for the wild game he brings our family each Sunday. I should see a flash of light and feel the power rise when they're switched on.

I see and feel nothing.

This is going to take some getting used to.

The wards make it so that the cabin is invisible even to magic folk and any noise we make can't be heard by the outside world. As soon as the wards are activated, he rushes over to the fireplace and stirs life back into the embers with a poker.

I remain in the doorway, watching him for a moment. His hunched body is rigid with tension and his face is bathed in a thin sheen of sweat. This isn't the Broin I'm familiar with at all. He's always calm and in control, silent but watchful.

He turns to me, his eyes gleaming in the fire light. "What happened to you?"

I don't want to get into it, so I walk over to him and say, "I got lost."

I expect him to scoff at me, or to mock me; instead, he returns to the fire. "Well, thank all the gods of the underworld for that. If you'd been there, they'd have found you, too."

The blood drains from my face as I watch him poke through the ash. "What are you talking about? Why did you drag me away from the cottage? Why were all the lights out? Where are Redera and Grandma?"

Broin's eyes fill with tears. He gives me a sympathetic look and my heart clenches with fear. I don't like where this is going. Something isn't just amiss. Something terrible has happened.

"Ravyn," he says at last, his hoarse voice cracking. "I tried, but they..."

He chokes on the words and I flare up with anger. I don't like his look or his erratic behavior. I especially don't like that he's upset.

"Spit it out, Broin. What's going on?"

One of those tears falls, tracing a silver path down his tanned cheek. "Your family... They're gone."

I know my grandmother will be mad at me for renouncing Lucifer, but moving away so soon seems both abrupt and out of character. She'd yell - in sign language, since she's deaf - but not abandon me.

"What do you mean, gone?" I demand, twisting my face at him. A nervous panic ripples through my body. "Have they left the Draoich? Gone shopping for the day? Ditched our horses for an Uber into the mortal world? Tell me."

"Ravyn..."

"*What?*"

He breathes a deep sigh, his forehead creasing. "The Witch Hunters came. For whatever reason, the protections didn't work. They found your family."

The cold I was feeling turns to ice. My voice is small, barely even audible. "What do you mean?"

"They're *dead*! Elnora and Redera... the wolves..."

I collapse into one of the armchairs, my knees giving out under me. I'm scarcely and yet fully aware of Broin's words falling upon my ears. They echo with such conviction that I know in my heart what he says is the truth. As a Huntsman and Knight of the Wood, he swore on his life to protect my family. But now... now he says that they're gone. Just like that?

My head swims with the words and shock rapidly numbs my body. I lean forward and place my head between my knees, breathing in through my nose and out from my mouth. Bile rises into my throat, constricting my airway and an erratic sob escapes my lips. It's a mixture between a laugh and a cry.

"N-no, you're wrong." I choke out, my vision blurred with unshed tears. "You must be, Broin!"

Broin just shakes his head, and, reaching out a trembling hand, falls to my feet. He takes my head into his hands and presses our foreheads together.

This can't... be happening...

The Rosso Lupa Pack, whose alpha we slander as the Big Bad Wolf, has been hunting our clan for centuries. My three-times great-grandmother, Esmeralda Hemlock, tried to get the God of Light to end our clan's famine and keep everyone from starving. When that failed and she received no answer to her prayers, she offered a sacrifice to the Dark Lord instead.

That sacrifice was paid in blood.

Little had she known that the wolf she killed was also the only heir to the alpha at that time. Our famine ended and we began our history of dark magic, our worship of the Dark Lord instead of the Storyteller who forsook us. But the Rosso Lupa wolves swore their vengeance. They became Witch Hunters and slaughtered many of our clan. With so few of us surviving the ruthless witch hunts, our Dark Lord hid us from them with powerful magic. We were safe for generations.

Until now.

When he said he'd remove his protection of me, he also meant my family. He stopped hiding them because of my renunciation.

This is all my fault.

Broin, knowing nothing of what I've done, leans back to look at me. "I saw their hunting party, but I didn't think anything of it. They'd never seen your house before, so why would I think they'd see it now? And I didn't do anything. But then I heard... and then I saw..."

My voice is still small. Weak. Broken. "Shut up."

"I went back to help as soon as I heard what was happening. I swear I did. But I..."

"*Shut up!*"

He shakes his head, his dark curls brushing his shoulders. "They're still there, Little Red. I couldn't let you go back to the house. They knew there was one witch missing and they're waiting for you."

Fury rips through me and I leap to my feet. The dagger is still in my hand, and I grip it hard enough to make my palm ache. "Then I'm going to pay them a visit!"

"No," he says firmly, straightening up. "There's ten of them and only one of you."

I shake my head at him in disbelief.

This can't be real. This can't be happening!

If this is somebody's idea of a joke, it's a really fucking rotten one and I don't like it. I take a step toward the door, but Broin gets in my way, standing between me and the exit. His powerful body towers nearly a foot above me.

"I'm not letting you go." The sincerity on his face would have warmed me at one point. Now I want to push him away, hit him, or scream until my lungs bleed.

I bring the dagger up and put the tip against his chest, right above his heart. "I'll kill you if you don't get out of the way."

"Then kill me if you have to. I'm not going to live in a world without you in it, Little Red. I've already lost El and your sister. I'm not going to lose you too."

His stupid devotion takes my strength away; I drop my weapon hand to my side, where it hovers in frustration. My eyes sting with tears and I waver, my anger melting into grief. Even hearing my nickname fills me with anger and despair. I've always been called Little Red since I was an infant. Grandma said it's because of how much I look like Esmeralda. My twin, on the other hand, was given the name Big Red because of her big, doey eyes.

Now... now the nicknames make me want to burst into tears.

"Are they..." My voice cracks. I can't even say the words. "Are you sure?"

Broin shakes his head at me. "Ten wolves dedicated to killing witches. Do you really think your granny and sister can stand up to that?"

"Their magic—"

"Gone. If the protections on the house were taken away, it's quite possible that everything else was, too."

To my immense embarrassment and frustration, I

begin to weep. I turn my back on him, because I don't want him to see my weakness or my guilt. When Lucifer took my magic as punishment for abandoning him, he must have taken it from my family, too. His wrath at my ingratitude has cost me everything. No grandma. No twin sister to annoy me or steal my clothes when I'm not looking.

Gone. Just like that.

I knew our unholy lord was full of spite, but this... I wasn't expecting this.

He said I'd live to regret my choice. He was right.

What have I done...?

Chapter Three

Ravyn

I stare into Broin's fireplace for what feels like an eternity. Time seems to be mocking me now. Every prolonged second is heavier than the last; no matter how often I look at the clock above the mantel, barely any time is passing. It's like the universe is taking great pleasure in my torment.

I wipe my palms against my dress again and try to rub the goosebumps off my arms. My favorite red gown, hand-stitched by Grandma, suddenly feels itchy against my ivory skin. I'm not sure how long I've been staring into the fire. It's like I'm determined these stupid flames will incinerate the last few hours from my mind.

But I know such a thing is impossible. I need to live with what I've done.

I'm a monster.

I feel like I've been put under a hideous spell. My family is dead because I wanted to attend a different school. How could I have been so utterly cruel and selfish?

Tears burn my eyes again and in my exhausted state, I let them fall and slip off my cheeks. It should've been me the wolves found. Not my sweet old grandma or my perfectly innocent twin sister.

It takes every scrap of willpower not to run home and see the carnage for myself. Despite how desperately I want to disagree with Broin, he's completely right. Going back there, with no magic and a pack of loitering Witch Hunters, would be tantamount to suicide.

I might not *want* to be alive right now, but if I'm to avenge my family, I need to stay alive until the deed is done.

I turn to Broin, who slouches on the chair beside me. He hasn't moved either since he sat us both down again.

"How long until we can go back?" I ask, swallowing down my grief.

His eyes are misted with barely contained tears. "Before I answer that, I want you to tell me what you were doing at the altar."

Another stab of dread cuts through my stomach, forcing me to look away. "I didn't know this would happen."

While sitting here, his thoughts must have caught up with him. He wants to know what I've done.

"What...were you doing...at the altar?" he repeats through gritted teeth.

My bottom lip trembles. "You know what I was doing there, I've been talking about it for months." I turn my head toward him again. "I surrendered my magic, Broin. I went to the Dark Lord and told Him that I wanted to be with Redera, but I never imagined...I never knew..."

Before Broin answers, he snaps his head to the side and sniffs the air.

Whatever scent he's picked up, it isn't good. He's already at the door before I can blink.

"What can you smell?"

Broin looks through the peep hole in the wooden door. "They've set fire to the cottage."

My heart leaps into my throat. I push off the chair and rush over to him. Smoke seeps through the cracks in the windows and doors, wrapping around the cabin like a thick blanket. It's not enough to indicate that the forest has caught fire, but it's enough to know my home has been ravished by the flames.

"Stay here," he warns, gathering a burst of emerald magic into his palm.

"Do you really just expect me to wait here?" I argue, unsheathing my blade.

"I don't *expect*," Broin snarls, opening the door, "I'm *ordering* you to stay here until I know it's safe. Remember you're a mortal now. You don't stand a chance against the wolves."

I glare up at him, absolutely refusing to listen. We're not in the bedroom anymore! Everything I once held dear in life, every person, memory, laughter and tear, are being erased as we speak.

Because of me.

"Mortal or not, I'm coming with you," I say decisively, stepping onto the threshold.

I barely set my foot on the ground when I'm suddenly pulled back.

The door swings over and locks from the outside. Emerald flames swirl around the door handle, signalling that he's set an entrapment spell around the cabin. I could kick and punch the door until I'm blue in the face, but it's no use. I won't be able to get out of here unless he lifts the enchantment.

"Let me out, Broin!"

"Sorry, Little Red—" A blue light emanates from behind the door, "—but I can't lose you, too."

Anger surges through me, erasing the weakness that had been draining my body. I move over to the nearest window and Broin, losing himself amongst the smoke-filled trees, transforms into his raven. I watch him take to the sky, and my rage dissipates into all-consuming shame and guilt.

Broin is just trying to protect me.

He gave up everything to protect my family. He abandoned his clan, his coven, his entire life to fulfill the debt owed to my grandfather. When Broin was severely wounded during the Silva War, my grandfather took him into our home. Broin was just a druid forced to fight for a coven who saw him as another pawn in their game for power. His life changed the second my family took him in.

Even before our clan was cursed by the God of Light, my family were highly-respected healers. So I'm not really sure if it was fate or just luck that sent Broin to my grandfather that day. But I'm told he had managed to heal Broin by doing the unthinkable.

He brought him back from the dead.

No witch or warlock has ever managed to repeat the spell without cursing themselves. Since necromancy is a form of powerful magic with great sacrifice, not many dare to try it. But my grandfather did, and our clan leaders have despised our family ever since. They don't like to feel challenged. Those who do pose a threat to the ruling council, the Maleficis Invictus, usually get banished to Underland. My family have long speculated that my grandfather didn't simply vanish off the face of the earth. He was taken from us.

But despite my grandfather's immense power, there

was still a sacrifice to be made when Broin was brought back. Once dawn came the next morning, my grandfather found a raven sitting where Broin had been resting. He had unknowingly cursed his patient, and every day since, Broin has been forced to become a raven until the sun dips below the horizon. Only then can he choose to walk as a free man again. He wasn't exactly angry about it; he was just glad to be alive and vowed to protect our family ever since.

I lean against the window, allowing my thoughts to focus on Broin. Anything to take my mind off...

I clench my eyes and take a deep, shuddering breath. Ravens are harbingers of death and messengers of the underworld. The message they wanted to convey that day was a warning not to interfere with the afterlife again. Safe to say, my grandfather never did, and our family—in fact our coven—have been forbidden to perform necromancy ever again.

What's taking him so long?

I pace the length of the room, twisting my blade in frustration. When I hear a distant caw, I run over to the door, desperate to find out what happened. The magic evaporates from the handle and Broin enters not a moment later, his clothes covered in ash. The blood recedes from his face the instant our eyes meet. He looks as if he's about to be sick.

I tenderly touch his arm, but he pulls away as if jolted by the contact.

"Broin, it's... it's me."

He shakes his head, a savage line drawn between his brows. "The hunters set fire to the house. There's...there's nothing left. It's all gone. I'm s-sorry." He chokes on the last word, and an unbearable weight clenches around my heart, pressing in like a thousand hot knives. He blinks down at me, his eyes wide but empty with shock. I've never seen him so desolate before. "I'm sorry, Little Red. I failed you."

I reach out to touch him again, but something stops me and I let my arm fall numbly at my side. I want to hug him and tell him that everything will be okay. But I don't have it in me to say the words, let alone believe them. There's an emptiness in my heart and it's spreading through my body.

"We're going to get through this," Broin whispers, nodding to himself.

I nod with him, though I'm no longer paying attention. Flickers of light dance in the trees behind him. The fire. With the hunters gone, I don't see why Broin would stop me from going home now. It's not like I'll be in any danger. I take a deep breath, and finding my resolve, I slide by him.

I half expect a wave of magic to pull me back into the cabin, but nothing comes. I race out into the forest. The farther I run through the trees, the more I'm convinced the area is safe enough for Broin to let me go. Or maybe he's just in too much shock to stop me. If so, I should feel ashamed about taking advantage of him, but I don't. I really want—

—need—

—to see my family.

I need to see their bodies with my own eyes.

After that, I'm going to hunt every last member of the Rosso Lupa Pack and destroy them. I'll skin them alive and wear their fur as coats. I'll make them regret taking my loved ones away from me.

I give a hasty glance over my shoulder to make sure no

one's following me. I can't hear or see anyone. The only sounds are my black flats pounding against the earth and my ragged breaths cleaving through my mouth. Suddenly my exhaustion no longer exists as I run toward the fire.

When I reach our home, the entire building is engulfed in flames. Wisps of ash carry on the breeze and a thick trail of black smoke streams into the starry sky. The only part of the land that hasn't been destroyed by the fire is the ash tree beside our house.

As I step onto the path and slowly make my way over, I realize why.

I press my hands to my mouth and suppress the screams, but the sobs claw out in a vicious crescendo that shatters everything inside me. Why? Why did they do this to them? I choke on another strangled sob and my body seizes up with grief.

My frail little grandma, still wearing her fluffy pink dressing down, hangs from the tree with a noose tied cruelly around her neck. My beautiful twin sways beside her, though her mouth and eyes are wide open. She's looking right at me.

Chapter Four

Ravyn

Strong arms envelop me in a tight embrace. My screams wail into a warm chest, strangled by a fabric that smells of firewood and whiskey. I try to hold on to Broin's shoulders, to attest that I'm not dreaming, that this really isn't a nightmare, but my body liquefies within his arms. He rocks me from side to side as though I'm a desolate child and despite the wails wracking my body, I can feel his erratic heartbeat pounding against my ear.

"I'm here, Little Red… I've got you."

His words of comfort only increase my sobs.

My entire body shudders with them as he runs a hand through my hair, down my back, caressing me, whispering words that I no longer seem to understand.

My vision is blurred, my limbs like mush in his arms. I close my eyes, but all I see are my loved ones hanging from the tree.

I was the one who put them there. They were hanged because of my selfishness.

More wails tear out from me. I've never cried like this before. Hemlocks are strong and unyielding. We aren't supposed to show signs of weakness; our clan forbids it. Yet it seems that every emotion I've suppressed until now is rising to the surface and Broin tells me to let them out.

He also tells me that we should give our slain the farewell that they deserve.

I press my face once more into his damp chest, clench his shirt into my hands and nod.

With the fire raging around us, Broin prepares what little he can of the funeral. Our ceremonies are usually conducted by the High Priest of our coven, which in our case is Reverend Cassim Salvador. The ceremonies are attended by every member. There are rituals and protocols for everything. I know His Excellency will be livid to find out we did this ourselves, but to be honest, I can't find it in me to care.

I just want to say goodbye.

And then I'm going to hunt those wolves down to the last cub.

I look away as Broin approaches the tree. I know I should help take them down, but I feel rooted to the spot, unable to move or even say anything. I'm afraid that if I do open my mouth, I'll burst into tears again.

In the corner of my eye, I watch him hold their bodies and cut each of the nooses. The sound of his knife sawing through the rope is something I will never forget. He places their bodies gently on the ground. I struggle not to purge the contents of my stomach. They look so peaceful lying there. To think how they must have suffered...

At least the next part I definitely can't help with. I'm not a witch anymore and my blood is useless to the Dark Lord. Broin sets their bodies on a dry patch of grass and unsheaths his blade. He engraves a reversed pentagram into the soil, followed by the head of a goat at the centre.

Once the Dark Lord's sigil has been completed, he cuts a cross into his palm and squeezes his magical blood around the entire circle. The explosion of emerald flames crackle with sinister energy. My hair stands on end and goosebumps break out over my skin as I hold my breath, watching as the flames devour their bodies.

Broin squeezes more blood into the fire; I can see his mouth moving, whispering the final farewell to our unholy departed. I'm glad he's taken control of their funeral. It's not just that I'm not able to do it without magic. I quite honestly don't think I have it in me to do or say a single word right now.

As I watch the flames lick around their bodies, I vaguely remember that Redera hadn't wanted a Satanic funeral. She'd wanted to be cremated privately and have her ashes spread around the ash tree.

Little had anyone of us known she'd be hung from its branch like a pig left to bleed out in the slaughter.

The quiver in my throat catches my bottom lip. I'll be with them again one day soon. To make sure of this, I stay until the last flame has all but died and our cottage has crumbled into rubble and ash.

When the smoke finally clears, I see that Grandma and Redera's bodies are no longer there. Good. That means the ferryman has accepted them.

In Redera's case, she'll be escorted to the God of Light, since that's who she worshipped in life. My grandma will be over the moon when she finally gets to meet her beloved Dark Lord. As for me? I'm left to spend the rest of my life knowing that I caused their deaths.

If only I had known the true consequences of leaving the Church of Shadows.

I would never have left.

I would never have gone to the altar.

I would never have asked the Dark Lord to free me.

Is this his way of punishing me for that?

But that doesn't make any sense. There have been countless people who left our church without being reprimanded. And my grandfather, after the trial over Broin's existence, left our clan with no issues. Our concealment spell wasn't lifted then and the Witch Hunters never found us. So why now? Why here?

Unless it wasn't Lucifer who punished me in the first place.

Could the God of Light have done this? I'm a Darkblood, after all. The sins I've committed in my eighteen years are plentiful. Mortals often talk about their False God and how he's all about forgiveness and atonement. But if he never forgave Lucifer, his own creation, why would he forgive a spawn of Hell?

Maybe he wanted to teach me a lesson before considering my proclamation.

Me he wanted me to suffer from the get-go.

Is this what Lucifer meant about choosing the wrong path? He hadn't been referring to abandoning his church. He'd been warning me not to trust his enemy.

An even deeper sorrow plunges into me. Somehow, I manage to pull myself off the ground. I brush off the leaves clinging to my arms and legs. My dress is covered in ash and slightly frayed from running through the woods. I regret the damage that's been done to it.

"Little Red?" Broin whispers, and I jump, not aware he's standing in front of me, waving his big hand. "I'm going to do a quick check to make sure it's safe. You got your knife?"

I nod, unable to speak over the lump in my throat.

Broin shapeshifts into his raven and takes to the sky with a caw. I expect him to tell me to go back to the cabin, but our bond remains silent. I'm surprised that it's still there despite my lack of magic. He probably wants to give me some space. Prying into my thoughts will be the last thing on his mind because he doesn't want me to feel *his* pain.

The strangest thing of all? I don't have anything to say to my family. I could stand here all night and beg them for forgiveness but begging won't avenge their deaths. All it will do is make me hate myself even more, when I don't have time for that. I have a pack of wolves to kill.

A silver light winks in the corner of my eye. I tilt my head toward the trees, my heart racing at the thought of Witch Hunters. Broin would have warned me if there were more about, so that's not what I'm seeing.

I creep a little closer.

White flash, then gone. Flash. Gone. Then I finally realize what I'm seeing.

A white rabbit scampers through the thick underbrush, its fur showing through the branches in momentary glimmers. Finally it hops out into the clearing, its little nose twitching anxiously. It turns and looks at me with ruby-red eyes.

The eyes tell me this is no ordinary rabbit. It's a familiar.

What person sent their familiar to watch our cottage burn? Was it someone who wanted to pay their respects, or someone from a white coven who wants to gloat? I want to grab a rock and throw it at the rabbit when it stops and looks at me again.

I find my voice, ragged from all of the hell-forsaken

crying I've been doing. "What do you want?" I demand, my voice a harsh croak. "Get out of here or I'll kill you!"

The rabbit doesn't seem all that impressed. If anything, it's somewhat miffed. Apparently it just thinks I'm rude. If I can't even frighten a rabbit, how am I going to destroy a pack of wolves?

I need my magic back.

For some reason, I think I need to follow the rabbit. I take a cautious step, my right hand instinctively going to my blade. The rabbit scuttles back into the trees, leaving me alone in the clearing. The black smoke rising from the cottage still lingers in the air, and I need to get away from it. I can't bear to smell it anymore.

The rabbit actually comes back and looks at me like it's trying to understand what's keeping me. It rubs its paws over its ears, then rubs its eyes. The smoke must be getting to it, too.

It looks up at me. —*What you're looking for isn't here.*—

The voice in my head is a girl's, but I don't recognize it. She speaks softly, sympathetically... but not patronizingly, which would really piss me off. Instead she sounds like a genuinely concerned friend.

"Who are you?"

—*What you're looking for is at Everafter. But you don't belong there and your blood will run.*—

Well fuck if that isn't omnious.

I tilt my head at the rabbit. "What do you mean I don't belong at that school? Who are you?"

The voice giggles, and she says, —*You'll see.*—

And then the rabbit darts back into the forest, nothing more than a distant light swallowed up by the trees. I repeat what she said, trying to make sense of the words. What I'm looking for is at Everafter...?

How fortunate. That's exactly where I'm going to go.

"Hey, come back here," I call after the rabbit, following it gracelessly. I'm crashing through the bushes like a noisy human. Any normal rabbit would be scared shitless of me, but I see that this one has stopped. It's waiting for me, watching me like it can't believe what an oaf I am.

Same, rabbit. Same.

It leads me through the forest, speeding ahead then waiting for me, guiding me around trees and away from the cobbled paths that my family and some of the other witches in the wood have laid down. When it's much too late to turn back, I realize that the little bastard has led me back to the Devil's Altar.

For an ungrateful minute, I consider sacrificing the rabbit, just to see what will happen.

Then I realize that I'm not alone.

I catch the faintest whiff of sulfur and a hot wind blows through my hair. My skirt trembles against my legs like someone is shaking it and I feel off-balance. My head is swimmy again so I grab the altar to steady myself.

"Both hands, my dear."

I whirl around, twisting my face into a venomous glare.

Lucifer is standing there in his beautiful form again.

I wanted to fuck him before. Now I want to fucking kill him.

Like *that's* going to happen.

He looks at me with a mock frown. It's just a mask to cover his gloating. My family are dead because *he* removed his protections. The Witch Hunters found them because *he* let them. Maybe it wasn't Redera's god. Maybe it was mine after all... or was it?

I don't know. I don't know anything anymore!

I pull my hand off the altar and rub it against my thigh, trying to wipe away the contact.

Lucifer looks at me quizzically, one perfect eyebrow rising toward the curl that brushes his forehead. He adjusts the gold cloak around his naked body as if he has not a care in the world. "I thought perhaps you had reconsidered," he states dryly. "I came to hear your apology."

"You'll have a long wait. You're not getting an apology," I spit out. My grandma would be horrified but I'm too angry and too hurt to be respectful, even of my former Dark Lord. "You're not getting anything from me."

"Then why are you here?"

"I followed a rabbit..." I bite my tongue. I don't know why I'm even answering him.

He chuckles. "A rabbit?"

"I was hungry." The lie slips out before I can stop it.

"Ah. I see." He clasps his hands behind his back and strolls around the altar. How can such a beautiful creature be so cruel inside? So full of deceit? "You know that lies sing to me."

Fuck.

"You want your magic back, don't you?"

I lift my chin, projecting more strength than I feel. "Not if it comes from you."

"More lies." He smiles. "Keep lying, my dear. Keep *feeding* me."

Resisting the urge to attack the bastard, I stomp back toward the forest. The damn rabbit is still there, watching me. This time, I do lob a rock at it, and it blinks out of existence. I scream in frustration, and Lucifer laughs at me before disappearing, leaving me alone in the unholy clearing.

That stupid rabbit brought me here just so Lucifer

could gloat. I've never heard of him working through familiars before, but there's a first time for everything. Well, if he thinks I'm just going to come crawling back to him after this, he's got another thing coming.

I will never beg him. I will never apologize.

I will never worship any god again.

Leaves rustle behind me, stirring the silence. A stronger whiff of sulfur burns through my nostrils. It seems to be coming from the Black Ravine. Grandma calls that area the forbidden zone because it was ruined by the war. It's mostly just spiky rocks, caves, and dead vegetation.

I wonder if that's where the wolves have been hiding all these years?

If they're in the Ravine, I'm going to find them and slit their fucking throats for what they've done.

After many failed attempts, I manage to find my way to the Black Ravine. I climb over the boles of fallen trees and uneven rocky patches that seem determined to impede my progress. The trees are getting older and larger the closer I get to the ravine, and the stench of sulfur is stronger. Something unpleasant and unnatural is happening. I don't need magic to tell me that. It's like a rain cloud swelling in the sky, ready to pop any second.

The ground has a sloppy, wet patch just before the gorge falls away. The river that cut this channel through the bedrock is still running at the bottom and I can hear the water as it moves. That river is part of the boundary of Draoich, keeping the other kingdoms apart. I wonder what would happen if I tried to cross. Knowing my luck, I'd probably drown or get struck down by lightning. Wouldn't that be a way to end this night? Struck down by the Storyteller.

I step on rocks to avoid the mud and as I do, I can see three very clear sets of boot tracks. Broin had said there were ten hunters, but I can only see three different tracks. They're fresh, judging from the edges of the prints. The water hasn't had time to soften them yet. The boot heels all have the image of a sunburst carved into them, leaving tell-tale marks where their wearers have walked.

Witch Hunters. I knew it!

The wolves are hunting in human form, which makes them easier to see and easier to catch up with. I follow the tracks, careful not to step into the soft earth myself. I manage to keep somewhat light on my feet, so at least that's one thing that Lucifer didn't manage to take from me completely.

I hate him. I'll never worship him again.

The tracks lead to a sloping natural ramp that runs directly to the mouth of a tiny cave. There's a fire burning in front of the rocky entrance; that's where the sulfur smell is coming from. There's a bundle of something in the flames, letting off putrid smoke. I've smelled that nasty combination of rotten eggs and manure before and it confirms what I already know. These are professional Witch Hunters who came armed with a ritual that's designed to dull a witch's senses. Any witches in the area that stinking cloud reaches will get woozy and sick and it makes it so much easier for the hunters to sneak up on us.

That's what these assholes think, anyway.

Grandma used to dose us regularly with similar foul-smelling herbs, training us to keep our senses when the smoke rolled in. She was wise, so very wise, and I honestly don't know how I'm going to get through the rest of my life without her and Redera. That gutted feeling returns, but I don't have time for it now. The enemy is close.

I follow the tracks around the campfire and its noxious fumes, then toward another stand of old growth oak trees that shadow the Black Ravine. Then, at the foot of the largest tree, the tracks just… disappear. There's no sign of them leading into the cave either. I'm sure I'm missing something, so I bend down to brush away some fallen leaves, just in case.

Big mistake.

Something hits me hard on the back and sends me sprawling.

My head slams into the tree, the bark ripping through my skin, and I feel a sudden pressure in my lower back. The pressure releases as abruptly as it came and I hear my dress ripping. Almost immediately I'm flooded with pain and I realize that I've been stabbed.

Blood oozes down my back, sending rapid shocks through my nervous system. My eyesight dims and my head turns woozy, causing my hands and feet to tingle in an almost deliriously funny way. It's the adrenaline kicking in.

I roll onto my side, my back against the tree, and look up into the sneering face of a witch hunting wolf. He's pus-plug ugly and if I had my power, I'd toast him here and now. Instead, I have to try to ward off his attack with my dagger.

It's not enough.

He comes close and two of his buddies drop down out of the tree to give him backup. I slash the first guy, catching him in the throat and he falls with a gratifying gurgle.

"There's more where that came from," I growl at them, pointing my dagger at the other hunters. My trembling hand makes the blade shake; they grin at me, knowing that I'm injured and afraid despite my damndest to hide it.

I never intended to find the wolves tonight and I certainly never planned on killing them by myself. I just wanted to find their hideout so Broin and I could return and slit their throats while they slept.

Why didn't I wait for Broin?

Because you're stupid and impulsive, a stronger voice snarls at me.

The hunters don't even bother replying. They just prowl toward me, their eyes flashing with a feral hunger that Witch Hunters have mastered over the years. I thought I was smart to put my back against the tree. Now it's preventing me from getting up.

In a series of blurs, the hunters kick me violently in the stomach and chest, driving the air from my lungs. All I can do is curl up into a ball to lessen the damage until I can breathe again. A rock digs into the kidney that hasn't been perforated yet, just to compound the suffering.

One of them has a gold dagger and he plunges it into my ribs.

I scream out, blood spurting between my teeth, and he pulls his blade free to stab me again. Before he strikes, I return the favor, burying my dagger in his stomach as much as I can. I twist and shove the blade through his intestines, gutting him like a worthless piece of meat.

A black form streaks in from the forest.

With two effortless swoops, it lands straight on his face. I see feathers and talons, then my attacker is reeling away. Broin helps himself to the hunter's eyeballs and the wolf lets out a shrill scream. He's rolling on the ground next to his dead friend, but another wolf remains on his feet. He looks like he doesn't know if he should go after the raven that's attacking his buddy or if he should finish me off. He looks at me, then turns to attack Broin.

I manage to struggle to my knees. There's not much at the base of the tree that I can use as a weapon, but the rock that was bruising my kidney is there. It's big, and I need to use both hands to pick it up, especially since I'm bleeding out and in a world of pain.

With my arms and legs violently trembling, I just manage to heft the rock to about shoulder height, which is as high as it has to go to hit the skull of the wolf who's trying to hurt my raven. His head makes a sound like a watermelon being cut down the middle and he falls to the ground, listless and pathetic.

Broin turns back into his human form, covered in blood. It's dawn, so I know he won't be able to maintain it much longer. The curse will force him back into his raven form as soon as the sun rises completely.

He grabs my hand and holds me steady. "Damn it, Little Red," he fusses quietly, but the alarm on his face tells me he's afraid. We both are. "I can't heal you."

"I know…" Talking is an effort, and I wonder if I have a collapsed lung. "I know… what I need… to do."

Broin is too busy examining my injuries. I squeeze his hand and when he glances up, I'm surprised to find tears rolling down his cheeks. Before this happened, I'd never seen him cry properly. Curse, punch, spit, bellow from the top of his lungs, yes. Even a few tears. But cry like this? Never. He's in so much distress I'm not sure he's hearing me. If he doesn't pay attention, I'm going to die here.

"Broin!" He snaps out of it and looks at me. "Take me to the altar."

Chapter Five

Ravyn

I never give Broin credit for being as incredibly strong as he is. He runs through the forest carrying me in his arms as if I weigh nothing. I know he has to hurry. Sunrise is nearly upon us; he won't be able to maintain his human shape for much longer. Already he's starting to tremble. I'm afraid that the transformation will overtake him and I'll fall on top of him, breaking a wing or something. That would be a terrible legacy to leave him with.

Strike that. I'm not leaving.

It occurs to me that I could be dying, probably *am* dying; that even if Broin gets me to the altar before he becomes a bird again, my request still might be denied. I can't let that happen. I can't die before my family's killers are destroyed. I pray - actually pray - that Lucifer will give Broin the strength to get me there and that he will give me the strength to survive.

I don't even know if he hears me.

Broin bursts into the clearing and dumps me roughly on the altar just before sunlight pierces through the trees.

He starts to speak, but his voice vanishes into a raven's caw, and then he's standing on the altar at my head, his black feathers gleaming in the morning light.

"Go," I tell him. "Go on."

—*No,*— he says, his mental voice firm. —*I'm not leaving you.*—

"You have to. He won't come... if you're here," I whisper, on the verge of passing out again. "And if he doesn't..."

I don't need to say the rest. If Lucifer doesn't come, I'm going to die. Broin knows this...... and he hates it. With a squawk of defeat and anguish, he flies away.

I lie back on the stone, the coldness soothing my back. I wonder if my blood is now filling the tiny crevices that our sacrifices always filled before. My eyes drift shut and I fight to stay awake. I feel so weak.

A hot wind blows over my face and I know that he's here. He speaks; even though I can't open my eyes, I can imagine what he looks like, standing there in his golden robe with his mouth in that little smirk.

"Well, well. What have we here? Looks like someone had a rough morning."

A warm hand rests on my side, right above the stab wound. The skin prickles like it's going numb. *Am I dying? Is this how it feels?*

He answers my unspoken question. "Yes. You are dying."

"Help... me..." The words barely come out, a mere whisper that nearly dies on my lips.

I don't want to die. I want to avenge Grandma... Redera... want to help them... seek forgiveness.

I manage to push my eyelids open and Lucifer has never looked so beautiful. His scriptures do him little justice. He's surrounded by a halo of black light and it shimmers over his hair like magic. The annoying smirk on his face changes into a gentle smile. I'm surprised by how genuine and warm the expression looks. Maybe it's just wishful thinking. Maybe it's just another lie.

He bends over me and puts his hand on the crown of my head. Lucifer brushes his lips against mine. Instead of the overpowering sexual response that I had to him before, I feel warm and safe inside. I can feel energy like hot honey rolling through my body and it's comforting in a way nothing has ever been before. It starts in my head and spreads down, moving over my face and through my body all the way to my toes. By the time that feeling of warmth reaches the soles of my feet, all of the pain has faded away like a distant dream.

"Rise, Ravyn Hemlock of Clan She'ol, Mandrake Coven," he says. "Rise and live."

I sit up slowly and find even the tears in my clothing have been repaired.

I look at him, and he nods. I sigh and say, "Thank you, my lord."

My lord? He's my lord again... after what he did?

He offers me his hand and I accept it. It's all so civilized and genteel, like I'm a princess and he's helping me out of my coach. I put my feet on the ground and stand firmly, all dizziness and weakness gone. I pull my hand back from his as my old anger surges up in me again.

Lucifer strolls in a slow circle around the clearing, walking the perimeter with one hand out, brushing the bushes and grass that have penetrated through the stone circle from the forest that surrounds us. I turn in place, watching him as he makes his progress. His touch withers the plants. He could have done that to me, and he's showing me this to make his point. He can harm as easily as he can heal.

Don't I know it.

He finishes his circle and now he's standing in front of me. His robe has fallen open, revealing his perfect body in all of its sinful allure. He stands still and lets me get an eyeful, displaying his muscles, his thick cock, his heavy balls... He's everything I could have wanted in a man. If he weren't a liar.

A villainous smile curves his lips. "Do you like what you see, child?"

I shake my head violently, though we both know that I very much appreciate the view. But I still have so much to ask him. So much to blame him for. So much to *hate* him for before I can learn to accept again.

"Why did you do that to me? Why do you want me to suffer?"

His smile fades as quickly as it emerged. "I don't want any of my children to suffer."

"You took them from me. My family." The words come out broken again, my voice cracked with pain. "My family were all I had left."

"I warned you of what chaos your decision would bring. You did not listen."

"*I didn't know*," I cry back at him, tears leaking from my eyes.

He is unmoved by my emotional display, as I knew he would be.

"You knew that your family were under my protection. What did you think would happen when you asked me to release you?"

I wipe my eyes, pissed off that I'm weeping in front of him. "I thought you'd remove your protection just from me, not from them."

He looks at me in disappointment. "Don't you remember how magic works?"

"Of course I remember!"

"Then you should remember that the magic that protected your family was put in place to protect your whole family, excluding none. I couldn't exclude you and still protect your family, could I? It's right in the pact."

Deals with the devil depend greatly upon the wording that's used. That's why so many incautious humans have been caught up in loopholes they didn't recognize, or didn't understand. Just like I didn't.

This was a giant loophole that left my family out in the cold.

I don't know what to say, so I decide that I can play spell lawyer too. "Is that pact in writing?"

Lucifer laughs. "How else could Esmeralda have signed it in blood?" He makes a gesture with his hands and a glowing scroll appears between them. It unrolls of its own accord and the words of the pact are displayed before me, along with my three-times great-grandmother's signature. The blood she used is still wet.

I read the pact. It's exactly what he says, and I see that he followed the letter of the law precisely. I look away and the scroll snaps back, rolling up like a window shade.

He dismisses it with a wave of his hand. "Now, then... What *else* did you want to discuss with me?"

I know what I need to do. He allowed my family to be killed, but technically he had no choice because of how our agreement was written. As much as it kills me, I really can't hold him responsible for that. It was my fault for not knowing exactly what would happen if I left.

There's only one way forward for me now. One future, one fate. I swallow down every bit of pride and honor I have and I kneel down before him, my head bent low.

"I beg your forgiveness, my lord. I offer you my allegiance once again."

His voice is hard, his reply instant. "No."

The word cuts through me like a cracked whip. I look up at him in desperation. "Please. I beg of you. I need you to forgive me so that you'll give me my powers back. I need them to hunt down the wolves who killed my family."

"*You* need," he sneered. "It's all about what you can gain."

"Yes," I agree. "In accordance with your teachings. Indulgence. Envy. Greed. I want them all."

He stares down at me and a slow smile starts to spread over his face. "So you want your powers back. What do you offer me in return?"

"I already said. I'm offering my allegiance."

He bends down and takes my face in his hand, holding my jaw firmly. He's not hurting me - yet. This close up, his eyes shimmer like liquefied gold. They're beautiful and terrifying at the same time. Hypnotic and insidious.

"I don't just want your allegiance. I want your soul. Every morsel of it."

"M-my soul? Why?"

His answer is to kiss me.

Despite everything in my being telling me that it's wrong, I could really get used to being kissed by Lucifer. Every touch of his lips fills me with fiendish desire and the sort of internal fireworks that only a really good orgasm can give.

Everything about him is sexual and it always has been.

Our magic is activated in sex. Our agreements are sealed in sex. Lucifer *loves* to fuck, with our minds and our bodies and so do all of his followers, myself included. I confess that I'm getting wet between my legs already and he knows that.

He pulls away, and I swear to Satan himself, his own eyes are filled with lust.

For *me*.

Underneath all that power and control, all that cruelty and divinity, there's also just a man.

The realization takes my breath away, even more than his kiss does.

"I will return your powers to you, Ravyn. I will even encourage you to avenge your family. In return, once you graduate Everafter Academy, you will live with me in Hell as my personal slave and entertainment."

He releases his grip on my jaw and crouches in front of me. His long cock almost brushes the ground and his thigh muscles are a wonder to behold. He could crush my skull between them if he so desired. He brings his face level with my pussy and I struggle not to squirm. I want to feel his mouth on me. I want to know if the Inferno's Kiss is real. It's not just your soul he can suck out. He can suck out the best orgasm of your whole fucking life. I hold my breath and look into his eyes.

"You will obey me - every whim, every breath, every order. You will worship and obey me absolutely and without question until the end of time."

None of these are conditions. They're orders... and it's driving me wild.

He reaches down and gathers up my skirt in his hand, his other one darting up underneath the garment to trace the wetness of my lips. He pulls his hand back and licks the fingertips, cleaning away the trace of me while his eyes are locked with mine. I shiver, filled with an innate, inexplicable lust for him.

"Do you agree?"

Lucifer's cock is getting harder and it stands as I look down at it, moving before my eyes. If a cock can be perfect, this one fucking is. Now I see why we worship him. I want to feel it fill every hole that I possess. I know what we're about to do. We're about to seal the deal the Satanic way.

The only way that I know.

I meet his gaze again. "I agree, My Lord."

He stands and pulls my skirt up to my waist with one hand while the other grabs me around the small of my back and pulls me close. The hot tip of his cock presses against my inner thigh and I spread my legs for him. He picks me up and impales me on his length, and I throw my head back in instant - fucking - ecstasy.

I'm no virgin. I've been around the block enough times to wear a path in the sidewalk. But Lucifer fills me like I've never been filled before. He's thick and long, hot and firm. He gives a sharp thrust and he's in me deeper than anything or anyone else has ever been and it feels as if he's growing.

I push his robe off his muscular shoulders and dig my nails into his skin, drawing blood. He hisses with approval, encouraging me to claw harder, deeper, which I'm all for.

He puts me on the altar and climbs on with me, bracing himself against the stone with his knees. Sweet unholy fuck. I'm being fucked by the Dark Lord himself. It's like a sinister dream wrapped up in a beautiful nightmare. All I can do is focus on him, his face, his eyes, his cock stretching and filling me.

Lucifer jerks his hips once. It's painful and sweet Lilith, I love it. He starts to fuck me, *really* fuck me, and all I hear is the rush of my pulse and the slapping of his body colliding with mine. He pounds into me, thrust after thrust, and I'm delirious with pleasure.

Just before I cum, he pulls out, leaving me whimpering and mewling for more. He turns me over onto my stomach and drives himself into my ass. The pain makes me gasp and then I explode, squirming and spasming in the biggest climax of my life. He fucks my hole ruthlessly, driving me into orgasm after orgasm, and I feel him getting harder and thicker inside me. My ass is sore and raw, unprepared for his entrance and brutal fucking and I love it. I love pain, like all of my clan do. I learned in Lucifer's name that pain and pleasure are much the same.

Now I'm getting that lesson repeated at His own hands; I've never been fucking happier.

I fall still for a moment, my arms and legs brushing the cold granite. But I'm not left like this for long. He plunges into me once more, this time so painfully I see stars – glorious, toe-curling stars. His thrusts are so hard that I can feel the soft tissues of my buttocks rippling with the power of his movement. It seems like my own flesh is vibrating against my clit. I've never felt anything like it. I've also never fucked a god before. I hear screaming; I realize that it's me as another dizzying orgasm builds up inside, forcing me to arch my back and dig my nails into the stone.

He stops moving, his cock buried to the hilt in my ass, his balls heavy against my pussy, which is dripping for him. He grabs my dagger from its sheath on my thigh.

"I claim you," Lucifer pants in my ear, bending to cover me with his body.

Then he straightens, still deep within me, and he cuts my cloak and dress away. With one huge hand, he strokes my now-bare back. His cock grows again and I feel like my ass can hardly stretch enough to take him. He moves so that he's crouching over me. He's transformed himself and his feet are cloven hooves. I reach down and caress the fur over his fetlocks as he begins to fuck me again. Moaning, I raise my hips up into the onslaught, begging silently for him to destroy me, to claim every inch of my body.

He happily complies.

He's fucking me so hard that my breath comes in gasps. My whole world is nothing but his body and mine and the way they're coming together. I'm bleeding, tearing apart from the inside….. and it hurts so good that I don't want it to end.

An entirely different pain stabs through me as Lucifer takes my dagger and slices into my back. He's cutting my skin, carving me. The blood drips down my sides, the feeling so erotic I can't stand it. My entire body tenses up and his cock twitches inside me.

Cut after cut, blood trickles down my back, and I scream into the altar, delirious with pain and pleasure.

He makes the last cut, and I cum *hard*.

I'm a quivering, gyrating mess, a tortured lump of happiness that he's impaled. He jerks inside me once more and then he floods my insides with his cum. It's hot, hotter than anyone else's and it's almost like being scalded, but not quite. The pleasure is unspeakable and I burst into tears from the sheer power of it.

Lucifer drops my dagger beside me and pulls free of my body. I want to reach for him, to pull him back, but

I'm so pleasure-drunk that I can't move. It's like he quite literally just fucked my brains out. Being a Satanist has never felt so good. Why did I ever leave?

I can see him picking up his robe and pulling it back on. With a wicked grin, he disappears, leaving me alone with the most profound afterglow in existence.

I'm just starting to come down from the climax when I feel it.

Magic.

It's suffusing through my veins, taking me from inside.

His cum transforms into pure magical energy and fills me up to the brim.

It changes me in ways I could only ever dream about.

I have *never* felt this powerful before.

I was always strong prior to losing my magic, but now I feel like there's nothing I can't do. I could pull galaxies out of the sky. I could string stars together and wear them like a necklace. I could heal any wound, cure any disease, cast any curse, even countermand the power of death. I start shaking, but not because of the sex and not because of the cold. It's the power. It's becoming me, and I know more than ever where and to whom I belong.

I belong to Lucifer.

It takes me a while to get a grip, but once I do, I gather up my tattered clothing and walk through the forest to Broin's cabin.

I know this place like it's my second home and in a way, it is. I often stay over and even have a chest filled with clothes. Those clothes and my mother's locket are now my only possessions. I took them for granted before. Now they're all I have to my name.

The slightest bit of air touching my back is excruciating. I can feel my magic healing the wound, but something is stopping it working completely. Another gift from Lucifer. He wants me to suffer for longer and I'm grateful.

When I reach the cabin, Broin is sitting on the windowsill. He flaps his wings when he sees me.

—*You're alive! I heard all that screaming and I was afraid.*—

I laugh at his dry tone of voice. "Why didn't you come and see, then?"

—*I couldn't.*—

"What do you mean, you couldn't?"

He hops toward me. —*There was a force field keeping me out. I couldn't get any closer than the edge of the clearing.*—

His tone is resentful. He knows those screams he heard weren't because I was in danger and he wasn't there to at least watch.

I turn around and show him my back. "Is it beautiful?"

He mentally sighs. —*Use the mirror.*—

I go into his cabin. On the inside of his closet door, he has a full-length mirror that he bought for me to use when I stay over. It was one of the sweet, spontaneous presents that he's always prone to give to me and Redera. My pure, untainted twin never made use of this mirror, but I've used it plenty of times. I know exactly where to stand so I can see my whole back. The sunlight through the window falls onto my still bleeding skin, bathing Lucifer's handiwork.

It's an inverted star, the upper points at my shoulders and the bottom point just above the cleft of my ass. In the middle, the goat's head is skillfully rendered; I'm astonished by the details and artistry that Lucifer was able to create. It's the most gorgeous piece of artwork I've ever seen. Lucifer has claimed me. I hate that I love it and love that I hate it.

"Thank you," I whisper to my Dark Lord. "Thank you... for everything."

I feel the slightest hot breeze and my ass tingles in memory. My power surges through me in one massive wave and I know that he is here, watching but unseen.

I grin at my reflection in the mirror. "Hail Satan."

Chapter Six

Ravyn

The next day, the tingling of the physical pleasure is only a memory and my emotional pain has come roaring back. To further torment myself, I've stopped by the cottage on my way to Everafter Academy. I wanted to take one last look. Although 'cottage' isn't the word to describe my home now. There's only a pile of rubble buried in the ash. Even the oak tree where Grandma and Redera had been hung has been burned into a husk. The flames must have caught the leaves after I left. It's razed our entire land.

It's all such a desolate waste now, just wisps left to float on the wind. This isn't my home or my life anymore. But it is a painful reminder of why I'm still standing here in the first place. I have only one job to do now, one goal, and that's to kill every last member of the Rosso Lupa Pack. Lucifer gave me my magic back for a reason and I plan to use it wisely.

The black stallion I'm riding showed up outside Broin's cabin a few hours ago. He was just standing there, grazing away in his halter and his saddle when I got up to look for breakfast. He's been glued to my side ever since and I'm pretty much convinced that he was a third gift from my Unholy Lord. He has to make sure I get to school on time, after all.

It's just past noon and Broin is in raven form on my shoulder. I must look quite the villainous part — a girl with her steed and raven. When I told Broin what the rabbit said in the woods, he thought I was crazy to trust an apparition. For all I knew it was just a spirit attempting to lure me into a trap. But then Lucifer spoke of Everafter, too, at the altar. It was practically one of his terms: graduate and then become his.

It doesn't seem like a big ask since I get to complete my mission in the meantime. All I want is to find the wolves and destroy them, one by one. To do that, I need to find their alpha. If you can kill a pack's alpha, you kill their cohesion and their will to fight. That's what Grandma always said. I'm convinced that the Big Bad Wolf is going to be at Everafter. What better way for a wolf to hide than to blend in with the sheep? That's what the rabbit was hinting at and that's probably why Lucifer was so insistent that I graduate from that academy instead of Nevermore.

I have every intention of doing this. There's just one little problem.

They're expecting Redera, not Ravyn Hemlock.

We are twins, so the resemblance between us is obviously strong. It's just a matter of a wiggle here, a glamour there and my appearance is now exactly that of my late twin, complete with her freckled cheeks. Before we set off for Everafter, Broin watched me cast the spell and put a permanency effect on it. With a nod, he approved.

—*I still approve*— he says. —*You look just like Big Red did.*—

My stomach heaves with guilt at the mention of her

name. Sometimes I wish Broin wouldn't eavesdrop through our bond.

"How about you search ahead?" I suggest, squeezing my ankles into Mephisto's side. The name was stitched on his saddle blanket, so I just went with it. He seems to like and answers to it, so, yeah. His name is Mephisto and I'm going to be his mom now.

Broin flies away and I guide Mephisto away from the cottage. Without a backward glance, we head for Everafter Academy.

It's time to hunt a wolf.

I'm so glad to have my magic again. I can see the schools beaming, one gold and one emerald, one in Fantasia and the other Draoich. The lights are supposed to guide those who belong there to its gates. Until now, I've never been able to see Everafter's light. If I'm to look the part of a white witch, I guess Lucifer gave me the power of one too. That explains why I feel stronger. He's given me white *and* dark magic. I have a part of my twin nestled inside me forever now.

I turn west and follow the paths twisting through the forest. The trees are taller here, but spaced out instead of crammed together and not quite as skewed. The leaves are greener, too, and the sunlight is able to bathe the ground in luscious golden hues. It's a stark contrast to what I've been used to all these years — the eastern side of the forest, where nothing new ever seems to grow and everything is trapped in darkness.

Yet there is beauty to be found in Draoich. The way the moon shines over the rocks and riverbanks; the moss winding around the trees like wayward blankets; the stars glittering through the leaves and spiderwebs; the crystal-clear water sliding into the Black Ravine. Darkness is all

I've ever known and witches like me have learned to seek beauty in the strange and unusual.

Admittedly, I am excited to see what Everafter will look like. I wonder if the surrounding landscape will look any different and if the school really is all it's cracked up to be. There's only one way to find out.

Beads of perspiration slip down my spine, sizzling against the wounds on my back. My magic has healed them for the most part, but the process is slow, which I'm happy about. Moving certain ways still hurts and reminds of what Lucifer has given me.

I shrug my cloak off and let it drape over Mephisto's hind. Up ahead, I see Broin cawing in the clear-blue sky and in the distance Everafter Academy sparkles behind him. We've finally arrived.

The academy is located in the sort of castle that you see in every fairytale book and movie. Gleaming white walls with blue tiled roofs. Four round towers on each corner, with a tall central spire over the great hall. All five - the towers and the spire - fly the flag of Everafter, which is a gold star trailing a rainbow over a white background, surrounded by a gold hem. How unbelievably twee.

Students turn to look at me as I lead Mephisto toward the stables. I'm obviously the last one to arrive and sitting on top of such a magnificent creature, I'm sticking out like a sore thumb.

A boy in all black gestures me to the nearest stall. There's no way every student's horse is kept in only three stalls. They must be under an enchantment of some kind. I guide Mephisto over, throw my leg over his withers and jump off.

"You better hurry," the boy tells me, taking hold of the reins. "She's already started."

He takes Mephisto into the stall before I can ask who 'she' is. As soon as they step over the hay-covered threshold, I catch a glimpse of what the stalls are really like, and they're absolutely enormous and beautiful. They're more luxurious than any home I've ever been in. I'm glad Mephisto will be living there. Hopefully that bodes well for what *my* room is going to be like.

I pull on my cloak, and that's when I see a tall, incredibly thin woman snapping her fingers at a crowd of students trailing behind her. Some of them are the same age as me and others a few years older. The latter must be seniors. They're wearing dark sweaters over white button-down shirts, tucked into either red tartan skirts that barely reach the knee or black slacks with cuffs. Everybody wears highly-polished black leather shoes, which probably makes the short skirt thing entertaining for the boys and girls who like to sneak a peek at what's underneath that plaid.

The newbies, like me, are all wearing their own clothes, which tells a lot about them already. Leather, chokers, denim and sneakers. They're definitely not what I imagined. I'll freely admit that I was being judgmental in assuming the do-gooders would be wearing polo shirts with sweaters tied around their shoulders.

"Seniors — make sure to control your designated groups," the woman calls over her shoulder, her ivory cloak billowing behind her. "First Years, remember to stay with your guide and please do keep up. The last thing I want to do is arrange a search party for blubbering students who get lost simply because they cannot follow instructions."

"Whoa. She doesn't seem very nice," a girl whispers to her friend, trying to keep up with the group. I fall into step with them, but I keep quiet. "She looks like she's been sucking on sour lemons all day."

I choke on a snort, trying my best to sound like I'm just clearing my throat.

"That's not very nice, Sirena," the girl next to her chides. Her voice sounds strangely familiar, though I can't figure out why. Her porcelain skin is swan-white, almost translucent and her short, pixie-cut hair is jet-black. She's small and dainty. "Although she does seem rather annoyed with us already."

"You think?"

"Who is she?" I ask the girls quietly.

The small, dark-haired girl turns to me, her sapphire eyes large and unblinking, reminding me of an owl who hasn't slept for weeks. "Mrs. Philomena Thornhart. Our Year Head. And who are you?"

I give them both a bashful smile, hoping to come across warm and, well, nothing like a villain. "I'm Redera and I have no idea what I'm doing here."

Sirena giggles. She's much taller than the other girl, and her hair is a vibrant shade of purple. In fact, everything she's wearing is purple, from her blouse and jeans, right down to her knee-length boots. Her eyes and lips are pale blue, like the ocean. "Join the club, sweetie, we've got t-shirts."

"I think our guide is over there," the other girl says, pointing to an exasperated senior trying to wave us over. "My name is Alice," she adds, her attention fixed on the senior. Heaven, I don't think she's even blinked yet. "It's nice to meet you."

"And I'm Sirena," her friend adds, looping arms with the girl, "her best friend. I've never met a Redera before."

"Ever heard of Little Red Riding Hood?"

The girls stop, and Sirena squeals. "No. Way! You can't be serious?"

"Oh, yeah." I smile at them. "That's me. Well, the new and improved version."

They exchange a glance and my pulse spikes in fear of what they're about to say. Was that a stupid thing to tell them? Little Red Riding Hood was *supposed* to be a hero, right? And no one, apart from our coven and the Witch Hunters, know we were cursed... Right?

"Should I tell her?" Sirena asks. "I want to tell her."

Alice nods. "Tell her."

I raise an eyebrow, and Sirena winks. "There's rumours that a wolf goes to this academy. How ironic is that? It's just a rumor though."

My jaw. Fucking. Drops. Just what I suspected! On my shoulder, Broin digs in his claws.

"Ladies!" Mrs. Thornhart puts her hands on her hips. "Are you coming? We're waiting for you. Chop, chop."

We hurry forward and she shoos us through the school's entrance. Students gasp in awe at the ornate furnishings. The rooftop is a dome with enormous hoops that rotate around each other, reminding me of the inside of a gilded clock. The ceiling is a mixture of clouds and rainbows that drift along an enchanted sky. Even the floor is magical. With each step, the illusion of rippling water spreads out beneath the elaborate tiles, making it look as if I'm walking on the ocean. Fish dart under my shoes and at one point, a massive blue whale swims by.

We're ushered through an open door and into an auditorium. The stage is empty except for a single podium, and the gas lights flicker and smoke. Our guide herds us toward the left side, in the wing seating, and we're more or less pushed into seats. I make sure I get the aisle. I also notice that I'm the only one with my familiar. Everyone else must have already been shown to their dorms.

The echoing clomp of hoofbeats sounds from the stage. A gray-haired centaur, his human part dressed in an old-fashioned professor's robe, comes into view. He walks to the podium, his tail flipping lazily. The students, who had been buzzing with talk and laughter, fall silent as he folds his hands in front of himself. He takes a deep breath, his muscular chest puffed out to the extreme.

"Welcome," he intones, his voice so deep I expect bats to be living in it... except bats wouldn't be welcome here, would they? "Welcome to Everafter Academy, where lessons are learned, friends are made, love is found and everyone lives happily ever after."

The crowd applauds and I try not to roll my eyes. The centaur continues.

"A hundred centuries ago, the God of Light, our Storyteller, created Draoich from the mist of dreams. He told the first story here in this Great Forest. He brought forth fairies and moonbeams and wishes that come true, and true love's kiss."

In the row ahead of us, a pretty girl with long blonde hair and big blue eyes sighs rhapsodically, followed by an intense yawn.

"Let me guess," I whisper. "Sleeping Beauty?"

She turns around to glare at me. "My name is Aurora," she informs, as if I should have known that already. "Don't forget it."

I shrug. "I'm trying to think of a reason to remember it."

"Ssh!" Mrs. Thonrhart says, frowning. Aurora looks back at the stage and I decide I might as well, too.

A huge golden eagle swoops into the auditorium and

perches on a chair beside the podium. I swear that chair wasn't there a minute ago. I don't sense any translocation magics, but I do see a team of brownies running off stage left. I guess they're the crew for this production. The centaur keeps talking.

"All was well. All were happy. But then... disaster."

He takes another big breath and the simpletons around me are hanging on his every word. It's like they've never heard anybody tell a story before. I cross my arms and my legs, forgetting in my impatience to act the way my twin would. Broin squeezes me with his talons again and I remember who I'm supposed to be. I unfold my arms and try to look just as rapt as the students around me.

The centaur goes on... and on... *Sweet Lilith, can he talk!*

"Darkness came to the Great Forest. A being of evil and hatred had arrived, someone who was jealous that all of the people here were living their happily ever afters. He was spiteful and he was cruel and he created the first villain."

Someone in the back hisses. It's a kid who has light brown skin that looks like it's made out of wood grain. He has what looks like metal studs at his elbows holding his arms together. The students around him boo.

"The Lord of Darkness had arrived in Draoich and he brought with him the very first instrument of chaos - the first Red Riding Hood."

Not too subtly, Alice and Sirena turn their heads and look at me.

Well, this is special.

"Red Riding Hood turned to evil. She slaughtered an innocent wolf, Lucius Rosso, and offered his blood to her dark god in return for powers of evil magic. Because of her, there was someone who was denied their happily ever after, because her intended mate was now slain. And so villainy came to the land."

The students react predictably, with jeers and whistles. Sirena and Alice are still staring at me. I resist the urge to put a hand over my face. An even stronger urge wants me to tell them all how the story really goes, as far as I've been taught. What my grandmother did was a sacrifice, yes, but she'd done it to save her clan from starving. That's not villainy in my storybook. That's just being pragmatic.

"Heroes and villains cannot co-exist, and the great Silva War broke out. We were attacked viciously, and we fought valiantly although many lives were lost. The Storyteller decreed that we should be separated. Heroes came here to the Western Wood, where the sun shines and life is beautiful. The villains were sent to the Eastern Side, Draoich, where the landscape is as dark and twisted as their souls. Nevermore Academy was built as a place where the evil and dark-hearted could be taught the ways of evil. And for us? For us, the Storyteller built Everafter here in Fantasia."

The room explodes in applause. I clap, too, but probably not as enthusiastically as I should. Some of the students are going out of their minds, screaming and clapping and waving their hands. I have no idea what's wrong with those people.

The centaur lets the nonsense continue for a while, basking in it, then holds up his hand. The room falls quiet again, but there's an undercurrent of excitement. On the stage, the eagle is scanning the room. It looks at Broin pointedly and I feel him hunker down beside my ear, making himself a little less obvious by hiding in my hair. That eagle is so big it could have a raven lunch and still have room for dessert. I reach up and stroke Broin's feathery chest. *Not on my watch.*

"And so here we are, guided by the Storyteller. We have gathered here to learn the best and whitest magic, to do only good. We are here to be honorable, gallant, noble and true. We are here to love with purity matched only by the finest gold. We are here to win our happy endings."

The crowd applauds again, but this time it's not quite as manic.

"I now give you Headmaster Dane Lockwood with his welcoming address."

A man in a silk suit steps out from backstage. I can tell right away that he's a dominant male. He's big and broad, with wide shoulders that look like they're trying to stage a jailbreak from his black suit coat. His waist and hips are narrow, giving him that delectable upside-down-triangle look that men's bodies have. His dark hair is cut conservatively, but it curls anyway, and he has a carefully trimmed black beard. He faces the students with a pair of piercing blue eyes and fuck if he's not the most beautiful unsullied man I've ever seen.

I scowl at my train of thought. I'm not supposed to think the unsullied are beautiful. Villains shouldn't want to bang the heroes; it goes against nature.

"Students, staff, faculty and guests," he beings in a deep, clear voice. His tone is like caramel and chocolate got together and had a baby. "Welcome to Everafter Academy. Look around you."

The students look around. Sheep.

"You have been seated in four sections. On my far right are the sophomores, ready for their second year of studying the magical arts."

The sophomore class gives themselves a round of applause.

"On the right center, we have the juniors, year three of

the magical arts. The most difficult year is upon you, with some of the most challenging course work. Good luck."

They groan, but applaud anyway. I guess they're game.

"Next we have the seniors."

Predictably, the fourth-year students erupt into cheers, hollering for themselves. It's absolute pandemonium. After a while, Lockwood holds up his hand and they fall silent immediately.

That is control.

That is sexy as fuck.

"You seniors are about to conclude your time with us here. You're almost ready to go out into the world to right wrongs and slay dragons."

The students go wild again and I frown. I've met dragons quite a number of times. They're not all that bad. They're just misunderstood and certainly don't deserve to have this lot going out to try to kill them. I cross my arms again. Magic folk who kill for enjoyment sicken me. It makes them no better than the animals they claim humans to be.

"And last, but not least, we have the freshmen."

The people around me clap, and some boys in the front row let out a fake wolf howl. Lockwood gives them a look so cold that I'm astounded they don't turn into ice cubes on the spot.

"You are welcome here at Everafter. If you have not already learned it, you will be taught magic, history, self-control and honor. Be warned: we offer a great deal, but we expect a great deal in return. You are embarking on what will be the most amazing experience of your lives, but make no mistake. It will also be the most difficult."

Yeah, I don't think so. No school could be worse than what I've had in just the last week.

Lockwood's eyes fall on my face. They're like sapphire jewels that cut right into me. I feel like he can see right through my disguise, maybe even to my soul. I'm pinned like a butterfly in his hand. I stare back. After a moment, he looks away.

Score one for my side.

I've always been good at staring competitions. The perks of mastering and totally owning Resting Bitch Face, I suppose.

Lockwood continues. "Go forth, students. Everafter is your home now. Make us proud."

The headmaster leaves the podium. The centaur returns, says something to the guides and before I know it, our own guide is ushering us back out of the auditorium.

We're led into the foyer again. There's a giant sea turtle floating across the ceiling now. Our guide — I think I heard Sirena call her Marcin — leads us toward the grand staircase. The guides signal each other and we break off into two groups led by two seniors. I slowly climb the granite steps. It's so surreal to think this is exactly what my twin would be doing if she were still alive.

"Are you the real Red Riding Hood?" Alice asks me in a whisper. Sirena takes the stairs two at a time and hurries after a dark-haired boy who looks every part the dashing young prince.

"No," I reply quietly, "but I'm not sure the school will believe me if they find out."

She nods absently. "Don't worry. Your secret is quite safe with me."

I'm relieved to hear those words. There's something so strangely familiar about this girl. It's like I've met her before, but I'm just not sure where. Maybe one of our coven's ceremonies? But she doesn't look, or even smell, like a witch.

—*She is a bit of an oddball,*— Broin says.

I smile and think back, —*Yeah, but the best people are.*—

Marcin leads us down a stone hallway supported by columns wound in gold ivy. At the other end, there's a wooden arch and we're shepherded through. The walls and windows are circular, covered by heavy white drapes, and there's the biggest fireplace I've ever seen on the middle of the floor. Velvet armchairs, sofas and ornate furnishings decorate the room. It looks more like royal private quarters than a student common room. Not that I'm complaining, but I do wish there was more black decor than the same white, gold, or light colors. They're beginning to give me a headache.

I'm surprised to find there are pool tables and game machines at the other end of the room. There's even a WiFi zone with flat-screen computers, which is rare in the Great Forest. The internet is more of a human thing and I can't say that I've ever touched it. Is that the shiny screen thing? Do I use a wand and whisper open sesame to get it to work? I have no idea.

Our coven aren't really familiar with modern day creations. We prefer to do things the old way, like riding horses and reading books as opposed to driving cars and watching television. Horses are still the main mode of transportation in the forest. That's mostly to do with convenience, since trees and paths are often too narrow to fit cars.

Redera did buy a radio once that we played in Grandma's kitchen. I guess it's really just up to the individual witch, or magic person, if they want to experiment with technology. The academy probably endorses them because it's easier for a lot of the students. Even now, some of them are on their cell phones, taking pictures or typing furiously.

Marcin points to the archways at either side of the room. "Boys' dormitories are on your left, girls' on your right. I'm sure you already know that since you've unpacked, so... what are you waiting for?"

With that, the group disbands with an excited bustle. Some of the boys cross the room to their staircase. Alice and Sirena motion me to follow them to ours.

"Have you found a room yet?" Sirena asks. I swear her hair has changed colour. It's now a deep red instead of purple.

Broin flies through the arch and up the stairs, probably to check that it's safe. I don't think he'll ever stop protecting me.

I shake my head. "I got here late, so I'll probably just take what's available. Fair is fair."

Alice seizes our arms at the bottom of the stairs. "You can share with us! We have another bed in our quad. There's usually four in each room, but we took the last one that only had three. It's like fate!"

Fate... or Lucifer is heaven bent on keeping an eye on me.

I'm just a witch with a deep, dark secret and a lust for revenge. I didn't have any special powers before he took them from me. What could he possibly want with me? Why does my soul appeal to him so much?

The weirdest thing about that? Lucifer has owned my soul since the day I was born into the coven. For the life of me, I can't understand what makes things so different now.

Chapter Seven

Ravyn

Our quad is thankfully more subtle than the common room. The interior isn't as bright and there are bursts of black and royal blue dotted around the spacious room. The drapes and bedding are mostly black, much to my relief, and crystals gleam across the ceiling like a sea of stars. One of the girls must have cast magic on them, but who? Neither of them smell like a witch.

I look around the room, searching for the vacant bed. There might only be three of them in this quad, but they're generously spaced out. I find Broin perched on the middle one pushed up against a large window. I can see a lake in the distance, nestled among towering oak trees soaked in sunshine. I find it sweet that the girls wanted their unknown room mate to have the bed with a view.

The beds at either side of me couldn't be any more different. One is completely girly and the other is a gothic black. Night and day. I have a hunch the latter belongs to Alice. It's shrouded in dark blankets that remind me of the dens Redera and I used to make in our room at night.

No, don't think about her.

I push those thoughts aside and go over to Broin. He hops onto the bed post and I give him a little scratch.

—*Everything seems okay so far.*—

—*Glad you approve, Daddy Broin.*—

He makes a gurgling noise in the back of his throat, frustrated that he can't shift into a man to kiss me. Calling him Daddy always drives him mad during our sessions. Heaven knows how we'll be able to have them here.

"Do you have any luggage?" Sirena asks, flopping down on her bed. Her hair is purple again, matching her bedsheets. The black coverlet draped over the bottom of the mattress is covered in shimmering scales.

"Actually, I..." I trail off, a little embarrassed to admit that what I'm wearing is mostly all I have left. "I don't have a lot. Just Broin here, my horse, Mephisto, and some dresses." When they share a worried look, I hurriedly add, "But I'm totally gonna make some more once I've mastered the weaving spell. So don't worry. Please. I'm all set."

Alice gives me an almost pitiful look, which I would usually despise, but there's genuine concern behind it that warms my twisted black heart.

Sirena, however, pushes off her bed. "We can't have that."

She digs underneath her blouse and brings out a pearl necklace. A heart-shaped shell gleams in the light. But then the shell starts to move, and I realize that it's actually a small turquoise crab. Sirena sets it on the floor and gently rubs its shell as though a genie's about to pop out. I hope not. Genies have foul temperaments.

"Come on, Augustus. I need to do something important. Don't leave me hanging."

The crab extends its eyestalks and its beady red eyes

latch on to me. Broin caws and after a moment, the crab opens its shell. I'm not sure what he told the crab, but it worked.

A blinding light emerges from the shell, and then Sirena just... jumps into it and the light evaporates like it's been closed with a lid.

I stare down at the crab in disbelief. "What did you do?"

Alice opens her mouth to reply, but then the light returns and Sirena is transported back into the room. Seaweed clings to her slightly wet hair and Alice clears her throat, nodding to it.

Pulling the seaweed out, Sirena hands me a box. "I think we're about the same size. But if not, maybe you can work some magic on them?"

I take the box from her, stunned by what just happened, and lift the top. I find a selection of clothing neatly folded and waiting for me. They smell like seasalt. I close the lid and hold the gift to my chest, a little lost for words. No one outside of my family has ever been nice to me. I'm a Darkblood. Everyone who isn't a villain is prone to despise us. It's inherent. But this...

"Thank you. I really don't know what to say."

"Just tell me you'll hang on to them until you're on your feet," she says, sitting back on her bed.

I nod, swallowing the lump in my throat. "Thank you so much. This... means a lot to me." My ears feel like they've caught fire from the blush rising to my cheeks. I'm honestly just surprised and grateful. Is it normal for strangers to give things without expecting something in return? "I'll give you them back as soon as I'm able to conjure clothes."

She waves a dismissive hand at me. "Barnacles! I'm totally cool with sharing my stuff with people I like."

"But you hardly know me," I say quietly.

"Well..." She shrugs. "We like you, don't we, Ally?"

Alice nods, climbing onto the end of her bed. "Oh, yes. You're peculiar like us."

"So let your freak flag fly, baby," Sirena adds with a laugh, dragging another bit of seaweed from her hair.

"How were you able to do that?" I nod to her necklace, which is now on full display around her neck.

Sirena quirks a paper-thin eyebrow at me. "We all have our secrets, Red."

Alice giggles under her breath, telling me these girls have a lot of skeletons in the closet. My kind of people, for sure. "Students aren't allowed to access portals on school grounds," she explains. "But Sirena's familiar has the ability to translocate her back to her kingdom at will."

"Kingdom? Are you a princess?" I ask Sirena, genuinely intrigued. I know this academy will be crammed full of princesses and princes, but honestly, I never expected someone so fucking cool to be one of them.

"You make it sound easy," she grumbles at Alice, then gently kisses the crab on his shell. His little red eyes are still pinned on me. "I'm from Poseida. Yeah, that means I literally sleep with the fishes." She nods to the box in my arms. "What do you think? Are they okay?"

I blink, hugging the box to my chest. "I'm sure they're beautiful."

And much too nice for me, I nearly add, but I don't want to offend her generosity. I might not be used to this sort of kindness, but that's not an excuse to act like a rude ass bitch. These clothes are at least enough to see me through autumn. I lied when I said I could conjure clothes. That was Grandma's forte, not mine.

"Well, one does try to maintain a good sense of style," Sirena says, fluffing her hair dramatically.

—*Oddballs*,— Broin mutters, —*the pair of them.*—

I give him the stink-eye. —*I like them, and my job is to blend in, right?*—

—*Right*,— he sighs. —*I just don't want you to trust every single person you meet here.*—

There's a knock on the door, seizing all of our attention.

An older girl peeks her head into the room. "Sirena, there's a boy waiting for you in the common room. He says it's important."

"It must be Erik," she says, smiling at the girl. "Tell him I'll be down in a flash."

The girl leaves and Sirena jumps off her bed. I watch her rush across the room to the en suite. The tap goes, teeth get brushed, perfume sprays and then she comes out.

"Well. How do I look?"

Oh, she's asking me.

"Hot as fuck," I say, and she laughs.

"Thanks. Wish me luck!"

"Good luck," we call after her, but she's already out the door before we finish.

"Who's Erik?" I ask casually, setting the box down on my bed. I sit beside it and start to fish through the clothes. Silk pyjamas, lace tops and dresses, chiffon blouses, leather and denim pants. All of them scream money. And she gave them to me for nothing? I'll need to repay her somehow.

"Prince Erik of Aira is her boyfriend. They... are off and on a lot. You will see. It's kind of their thing." She comes over and sits next to me. Scrunching her nose at the faint smell of salt, she probes, "What about you? Are you dating any princes or princesses?"

I don't know about dating, but I did just fuck the Prince of Darkness last night.

Broin must have been reading my thoughts, because he flaps his wings and gurgles again. This time it sounds more like a laugh.

—*Stop reading my thoughts, you naughty boy!*—

—*Boy?*—

—*Fine. Daddy. Whatever.*—

—*You'll pay for that tone of voice later, young witch.*—

"No, I'm not dating anyone," I answer her question, smirking at what Broin just promised, "and I really don't plan to be."

"Oh. Did you have a bad experience?"

"Umm..."

I think on that, surprised by her forwardness. The cynic in me has never wanted to get my heart broken, so I've only ever had physical relationships with members of the clan. If I don't let anyone in, no one can hurt me. I suppose Broin has been the one exception. Oh, and my 'unconditional love' for the Dark Lord. But then I decided to break things off.

That ended well.

Not.

"I guess you could call it that," I answer, shrugging. "What about you?"

She reaches over and grabs hold of the black lace dress I just had my eye on. "This would look amazing on you."

I blush. "Thanks. It is beautiful. I'm worried I'll ruin it." I lift my hands and wiggle my fingers. "Butter fingers. I'm always falling over and doing something stupid."

Alice smiles and sets the dress back down. She looks

down, her long lashes brushing her dimpled cheeks. A fleeting sorrow flits over her face. Since she clearly wants to avoid answering about her love life, I drop the question, not wanting to pry.

"About our classes... have the schedules already been handed out?"

She lifts her head, smiling again. "Did you break your scroll?"

"What do you mean?" I fold the dress back up and tilt my head at her.

"The scroll. You need to break it first to get your schedule." I watch her go over to the wooden nightstand beside my bed and bring out a scroll. When she hands it to me, the brown exterior reminds me of a fortune cookie. "Once you break it, the schedule will appear inside. Isn't that cool?"

I hate to admit it. "It's pretty neat."

We both hold our breaths as I gently bend the scroll at the middle. *Crack*. The shell falls away and inside, a white scroll appears.

I take it out and look over my classes. "Yikes. The first class is today, in an hour. Potions with Professor Rumpkin."

Alice peers over the box to get a better look. "At least you'll be with Sirena. What other classes do you have?"

She really doesn't understand personal space, but to be honest, neither did Redera. I grew to love that about her. In a way, Alice reminds me of my twin—the pale skin and the soft, slightly spaced out voice. Even her dark hair is a similar black that looks almost blue in the lights.

"Oh, you've got double Familiar Handling tomorrow." She points at the class titled *FAMILIAR HANDLING 1 - Professor Abdiel*. "I have that class too! We must be going into the forest. Sirena's big sister, who graduated last year and is going to be queen of Poseida, told me that the lessons are usually one hour long. If you have a double period, that means you're in for a surprise, unless it's exam time."

We both groan.

"Speaking of which..." I turn the scroll over but the other side is blank. "There's nothing here about our exams."

"Yes, those details will come later, usually two weeks before. I overheard Marcin say that we have exams every season. The Year's End Exams usually determine our next year's schedule. Some advance and others have to sit back and do the whole year again."

"Well, that stinks," I mumble, scanning my schedule again.

The classes don't look particularly hard. I just might be able to do this...

POTIONS 1 - WELL, I'VE BEEN MIXING DRAGON SCALES and toad livers since I was two. May Satan strike me down if I fail to live up to the Hemlock name.

FAMILIAR HANDLING 1 - I think I've pretty much got that covered.

ENCHANTMENT 1 - Bibbity bobbidy boo. Done. This is actually where I'm strongest. I wonder if the white magic His Unholiness gave me will improve that?

MAGICAL THEORY AND ETHICS - I know the basics, but most of my knowledge is about Dark Magic and Sinister Arts. This will be interesting, except for the ethics part. Snore.

CONJURING 1 - Now here I've got my work cut out for me. I've never been good at that. I can conjure food and that's about it.

ELEMENTAL CONTROL: EARTH - This is completely new to me and I honestly can't wait.

I scroll the schedule back up and grin at Alice. "What class are you most looking forward to?"

"If I had to pick just one it would be conjuring. That's what I love most."

"Hopefully I can learn from you. I'm terrible at conjuring anything that isn't food or tea."

Just as I say that, the door creaks open and a white rabbit hops into the room.

"There you are!" Alice leaps off my bed and runs toward it. She crouches down so all I can see is her back. "I've been looking everywhere for you... No, class hasn't started yet. I know. Don't worry. I'm not going to be late. Oh, stop nagging."

Straightening off the floor, she turns around with the rabbit in her arms, and suddenly something clicks.

The voice... the white rabbit... Surely it can't be?

Alice holds the rabbit out as if the poor thing is a sacrifice. If that's the same rabbit I saw in the forest, it almost was. "This is Jasper. My familiar. He's always worried that I'm going to be late."

I eye the rabbit curiously. He could just be any ordinary white rabbit, because even some mortal ones have red eyes. "Is Jasper also a Spirit Guide?"

Her arms fall by her side and she lets Jasper hop onto the floor. "How do you know that?"

"I saw him yesterday. Last night. He... guided me through the forest. He told me to come here. *You* told me to come here."

"Me?" I never thought it was possible, but she turns a whiter shade of pale. "Oh, no. It happened again."

Broin flies over to the rabbit and twitches his head from side to side, probably communicating with him.

I soften my voice, genuinely curious. "What happened?"

Alice sits next to me again. She ponders for a moment, and I notice she's flicking her fingernails off her thumb, her attention on Jasper instead of me.

"I'm not a witch. My parents, whoever they are, were one hundred percent mortal. But my great-great grandfather was a warlock and I inherited some of his power. My seer ability is the only reason I was invited to this school. The only reason I was allowed to... never mind. But my power isn't something I can control yet. I'm hoping Everafter will help with that." Her eyes widen into saucers. "It's rather exhausting."

I digest every word, including the part where she trailed off. There's a light feeling blossoming in my stomach. Hope, maybe, or excitement. I definitely saw Jasper last night and heard Alice's voice.

"What kind of clairvoyance is it?"

"Dream scrying," she answers softly, confirming my speculations. "Psychic navigation. Precognition. Astral projection. Every one of them. Too many for me to always remember what happens, especially when I'm asleep." She blinks, as if she's just joined reality again, and looks at me. "Last night, I dreamt of nothing, so I knew Jasper and I were in the spirit realm. But just like every other time, I forget what happens when I wake up. Today is the first I've ever seen you in real life. I'm sorry I don't have any answers."

The hope growing inside me withers. If she can't

remember why she came to me last night, or why she told me to come to this academy, I have nothing to go on. For now, at least. There's a reason Alice appeared last night, just like there's a reason I've become her roommate. Nothing in life happens by coincidence. While it might be unclear right now, I do believe there will be something to help light this path for me.

"Don't worry about it." I gently rub her arm, giving her my warmest smile. She tenses a little, looks at my arm, then relaxes and returns the smile. "We're going to be roomies for four years. I'm sure we'll find out the meaning of it all."

She gives a hesitant nod. "You know, I wish I could say that I love my power, but I don't. It keeps me awake while the rest of the world are asleep."

"I know that feeling."

"You do?" Her eyebrows disappear underneath her choppy fringe. "Are you a night owl, too?"

"That's one way to put it. I just...really like the moon."

Another smile from her and this time it brightens her face. "Sirena is like that. I have a feeling we're all going to be really good friends."

As if on cue, Sirena kicks open the door, dressed in a plaid uniform. I don't know where she changed her clothes. "Hey, my little freaks. Who's ready to make potions?"

Chapter Eight

Ravyn

I change into my school uniform. The skirt itches, but it shows off my legs to a nice effect. Most of the girls, including Alice and Sirena, are wearing white knee-length socks, but I opted for black, because, well, black is the color of my soul. They blend with my black shoes and make my already long legs look even longer. I enjoy walking past the boys on the way to class. Some of them can barely keep their tongues in their mouths. I take note of the ones who are the most interested. You never know when that will come in useful later.

Sirena stops before we get to the building. "Hold up," she says. "I'm going to get a drink of water. Once we get in there we won't be able to drink anything, just for safety's sake."

I shrug. "Sure."

"Go ahead," she smiles. "I'll catch up."

I'm not sure what I expected Professor Rumpkin to be. Maybe I'm expecting a canny little dwarf like Rumplestiltskin, or maybe something ridiculously cute and furry. I know for damned sure that I wasn't expecting.... This.

Clarinda Rumpkin is a fairy. An honest to Satan fairy. Blue gown, blue pointy hat trailing a blue chiffon scarf and blue gossamer wings. She's about a foot tall, maybe less, and she hovers and buzzes like a hummingbird. She's bouncing slowly up and down at the front of the classroom, her wings beating so fast that they're nothing but a blur when we file in.

She claps her tiny hands and calls out in a voice like a piccolo, "Places, please. Right away. Sit at the benches here at the front."

I head toward the first bench I come to. There's four chairs and only one is occupied. Just before I sit, the boy who's already there flings his leg across the seat.

"Saved," he says.

He's a little too good looking, with black wavy hair and hazel eyes. He's wearing a leather jacket with his school uniform, which makes him look like an idiot. He gives me the once over and a slow smile that I think is supposed to be sexy creeps over his face.

"I might make an exception, if you make it worth my time."

I roll my eyes and walk to the next bench. He's not worth *my* time.

Aurora, the blonde bimbo from the assembly, comes flouncing in with her equally blonde posse in tow. They look like they came from the same factory. Perfect faces, perfect bodies, perfect blue eyes, perfect everything. She sneers at me and sits beside the boy. Her girls sit down at the bench, too.

"Thanks for saving the best seats, Erik," she simpers to him.

He smiles at her and I can practically smell his ego from where I'm sitting. "No prob, babe."

Erik? I'm sure that's Sirena's on-again, off-again boyfriend. If she sees this, they're definitely going to be off again.

Right on cue, Sirena strolls through the door just as Aurora reaches out and flips one of Erik's dark locks off his forehead.

My roommate stops and puts her hands on her hips. "Really, Erik? *Really*?"

He looks startled to see her, but Aurora only smiles a little 'gotcha' smile at Sirena. This bitch needs to get hexed. Or axed. I'm okay with either.

Sirena walks closer, her eyes fixed on Aurora's smirking face. "You have until the count of three to get away from him. And let me tell you, my people are good with tridents."

Aurora tilts her head. "What's in that necklace, Sirena? Don't you know that we're not supposed to bring familiars to class?"

Sirena's face goes red and blotchy and I expect her to lunge for Aurora at any second. Professor Rumpkin interrupts what might have been an interesting cat fight.

"Now, now. Please leave a seat open between you, just in case of splashing. Prince Erik and Princess Cinder, please move to the bench behind."

Erik and one of the blonde girls stand up and move back, clearly reluctant, even though doing so saves Erik from being filleted by a mermaid. I'm a little disappointed. That would have been poetic justice. Sirena sits down at my bench, obediently leaving an open seat between us, and glares daggers at her boyfriend.

"Face the front, please," Professor Rumpkin chirps and she starts to flit around the room like an exceptionally fat blue bumblebee. "Now we're going to go over the syllabus and I'm going to help you identify all of your equipment."

Beaker, candle, retort, jar, cauldron, pipette, crucible, mortar and pestle. Got it.

Sirena mutters, "He's going to be nothing but chum if he keeps it up."

I nod approvingly, then settle down for the business of being bored to death for an hour.

It's actually worse than that.

It's not boring, it's absolutely insulting.

I knew more than the rest of the class by the time I could walk. I want to leave, but instead I sit quietly, pretending to listen the way Redera would. It takes a lot of self-control to pretend to be as good natured as my twin was.

Everybody around me is feverishly taking notes about the hardware and how it's used. Professor Rumpkin looks at me quizzically a few times, since I'm not writing anything, but she lets it go.

I wonder what she'd say if I told her my grandma had a potion that used fairy wings as an ingredient. Some potion ingredients can be a little grotesque. Well, for Darkblood potions, anyway.

It's a shame we aren't allowed to bring our familiars to class - except to Familiar Handling. I'm sure Broin would be keeping me more entertained than this class ever could. Why is she literally starting with the basics? We're eighteen - some of us probably only that in human years. This lesson feels completely unnecessary. Maybe it's more of a refresher than anything? I don't know. I just feel like I'm wasting my time here. But I *am* Redera now and I know she'd respect the professor and classmates enough to listen.

After class is finally over, we all walk out into the sundrenched courtyard. Aurora marches right up to me.

She's holding her books in her arms like they're part of a push-up bra, and her fountain pen is between her fingers like an inky cigarette. She knows how to pose, that's for sure.

"I noticed that you weren't taking any notes," she says.

Cinder, whose delicate hands are covered in equally delicate gloves, backs her up. "Yes. Why didn't you take notes?"

Another prince ambles over, tall and fair headed. Now this is the sweater-over-the shoulders Biff Buffingham type I was expecting. "Maybe the poor dear can't afford a pen and paper."

"Maybe she thinks she's too smart for notes," Aurora ventures. She glares at me. "Is that it? Do you think you're too smart for Everafter?"

I am trying, *really* trying, to play the part of the good twin, but she's making it fucking impossible. "As a matter of fact, I am. I don't need to take notes on something I already know."

Cinder snorts, which isn't a very princess-like thing to do. "Oh, right. You already know it," she mocks. "I don't think you know anything."

Sirena growls, "Knock it off, you guys."

Prince Biff smirks. "Oh, is this your new girlfriend? Finally gave up on Erik and decided to switch teams?"

They laugh like it's the funniest thing they've ever heard. I notice Erik and one of his buddies standing nearby, not getting in on the bullying but not doing anything to stop it, either. Cowards.

I look at Aurora's pen and mentally check where it's pointing. The target is too perfect for me to pass it up.

"*Exspue atramento*," I whisper sweetly.

The pen explodes like a water cannon, shooting Cinder

square in the face with more black ink than its cartridge should have held. The black splat covers her face like she's the guest of honor at a bukkake party. It drips onto her blouse and gets in her hair, staining the blonde strands. For a heartbeat, she stands in stunned, horrified silence, and then she starts to *scream*.

A hawk streaks down at my face, only to suddenly be intercepted by Broin, who's cawing up a storm, probably cussing the hawk out in every language known to familiar kind. He's supposed to be in my room but he must have sensed my annoyance. Aurora shakes the pen in my face.

"Did you do this?" she demands. "*Did you do this?*"

"Sure did, and I can do it again. Watch where you're pointing that thing. You just never know if a witch is watching."

She looks uncertain, then lifts her chin. "I don't think you can cast something like that twice. You're not that powerful. You're just a basic witch."

Oh, that's rich. I throw my head back and laugh. This time, I don't even bother with anything as obvious and showy as magic words. I just poke my finger toward her. The pen bursts again, splattering her in the face and destroying her carefully-applied makeup. It feels good to cast small spells without my wand, especially on bullies.

Cinder's screaming has attracted a crowd of students and Sirena grabs my arm and pulls me away. The preppy prince takes both Cinder and Aurora and guides them back toward the dorm. One of the guys next to Erik, another infuriatingly good-looking blond with a shoulder-length hair and a sweet round face, applauds and points at me with a grin on his face.

Sirena hauls me at speed out of the courtyard and into

the biggest building, which happens to hold the library and the cafeteria.

"Be careful!" she hisses. "That was awesome, but that's the sort of thing that Lockwood despises. He hates when people misuse magic."

"That wasn't misuse," I object. "It was pay back."

She rolls her eyes. "Spoken like a true Darkblood."

Her words stop me cold.

It's the first day and I've already blown my disguise.

I'm behaving like Ravyn, not Redera.

How does Sirena know that I'm a dark witch? And why doesn't she seem bothered by it?

Erik and his friend follow us in from the courtyard, hounded by a gaggle of idiot girls.

The blond says, "That was quite a performance. Are you a witch?"

One of the girls with him, another blonde with unnaturally long hair twisted into a braid, says, "Yes, because witches don't belong in Everafter."

"It's dark witches that don't belong here," I correct her, crossing my arms.

Sirena chimes in, also folding her arms. "White witches are still welcome the last we checked."

Despite the fact that she knows who and what I really am, she still has my back. This chick is serious best friend goals.

"Yes, Rapunzel," Erik sneers. "Didn't you read the brochure? Seems Everafter is letting just anybody in these days."

The blond boy asks once more, "Are you a witch?"

"Witches. Aren't. Welcome," Rapunzel reiterates, stabbing at me with her fingertip. "Only. Princesses."

"Well," I say, gesturing toward Erik and the blond, "that explains how they got in here."

The blond's face turns dark with anger and he stomps away. Erik and Rapunzel follow him, along with his little crowd of hangers-on. I let them go, because I absolutely do not care what pretty-boy, tiny-dicked princes think of me.

A bell near the cafeteria rings loudly, and I feel like my ears are going to shatter. Draoich was never this loud.

"What the he—" I catch myself before I say 'heaven', "—hell is that?"

"Feeding time at the zoo," Sirena shrugs. "Come on. Lunchtime."

I'm relieved she's reacting to my identity as though it's nothing. I do the same, hoping my dark heart won't cause a rift between us, and ask, "What if I'm not hungry?"

"Then you won't be able to have any food until dinner and we eat late around here."

She grabs my arm and pulls me into the cafeteria. It looks the same as any other cafeteria, with long tables and huge lines for almost-edible food cooked in mass quantities, using techniques guaranteed to scour all of the taste out of any ingredient. Everything's organic. This is literally my idea of heaven. Ugh.

I look around for someplace to sit and wouldn't you know it? Today's my lucky day. The only table with any open seats is the one where Erik and his friend are seated.

"Well," I mutter to Sirena, "here goes nothing."

We get in line and select the best options out of all the bad choices available. Something tells me that the kitchen staff isn't trained in the magical preparation of food, because it looks like everything is fucking boiled. I don't think I'll be eating much in this place. Good thing I can conjure up my own food.

I choose the vegetable soup and we go to the table with the last open seats, now down by one because Prince Biff - or whatever his actual name is - joins us. I guess food was more important to him than assuaging Cinder's and Aurora's egos. Good call, actually.

Erik executes his asshole maneuver again, covering the seat with his leg. "Reserved."

"For whom?" I demand, grimacing at him.

"For anybody who's not a dark witch," Prince Biff says, leaning over with a sneer. "Go back to Nevermore where you belong, *Darkblood*."

First of all, how the *fuck* does he know I'm a dark witch? Not that anyone here seems to believe him, but still, the fact that he's right pisses me off.

Second, who is this fuckpot?

I've had enough of it.

All of the upset and the frustration that I've been keeping bottled up explode and I dump my bowl of soup onto his head. He leaps up and I turn my tray into a weapon, pulling back to smash him in the face with it.

I don't get the chance to follow through.

A huge masculine hand grabs my wrist and then the tray is wrenched out of my grip. I spin around and find myself face to face with the delectable Headmaster Lockwood. Up close, he's even taller than I expected. He's an imposing physical presence and I'll bet that under his suit and cloak he's absolutely ripped.

"Uhh... hello there, Sir..." I stammer, my arm still held in mid air by one of his hands.

"What is this about?" the headmaster demands. The

intensity in his eyes is chilling and I nearly back up a step before I catch myself. I stand my ground and lift my chin in defiance. The anger in his gaze actually increases, sending an intense thrill through me. Ooh, that look does things for me.

To my surprise, Erik's other friend speaks up in my defense. "It was my fault, sir," he says, taking the blame for Prince Biff. "I was teasing her and she meant to douse me in the soup."

Lockwood looks at the boy and says, "Christopher, I'm surprised at you, and disappointed. I thought you were someone who was too well-mannered to get into this sort of trouble."

Christopher hangs his head and Prince Biff grabs napkins from the table to wipe his face.

"And you, Erik," Lockwood continues. "You are out of uniform. Take off that ridiculous jacket."

Reluctantly, Prince Erik complies and then the moment I've been waiting for arrives. The headmaster turns to glare at me and his eyes flash. "As for you, Miss Hemlock... I know that you haven't had the advantages that some of your fellow students have had, but that's no excuse to act like a barbarian. If I ever see you wasting food again, I will have no choice but to intervene."

That sounds like a promise *and* a threat wrapped up with a bow.

"Yes, Sir," I say, trying to sound respectful.

Lockwood puts the tray down on the table. "Get more food, since you spoiled this. And fetch a second-year to practice magical cleaning."

A girl nearby produces a wand and sweeps it over the area that's been drenched by my soup. The food disappears as if it had never been there, not even leaving a wet spot on Prince Biff's huge head. His face is still purple with rage.

Lockwood nods at the improvement before he faces Prince Biff. "I trust this will not happen again, Gideon?"

There's a long, strained pause before he answers. His eyes still glaring daggers into my skull, he growls, "I'm sure it won't, sir."

"Good. As you all were then." Lockwood stalks out of the cafeteria, his long cloak flapping behind him.

The room stays quiet until all we're sure he's gone. Gideon (aka Prince Biff), Erik (aka Leather Jerk), and Christopher share a silent look. Gideon nods once, then they grab their trays and stalk away.

"Sheesh. Did you see Lockwood's face? He's really pissed off," Sirena mutters, digging into her vegetable stir fry. "Watch your step, sista."

I can think of a lot of things with Lockwood I wouldn't mind watching, but my step surely isn't one of them. I know that look he gave me — I've seen it my whole life. There's something sinister about the headmaster, a string of dark energy that stretches between us. I felt it in my veins, calling out to the darkness within me.

Colour me fucking intrigued, things just got a little interesting. About time.

Chapter Nine

Ravyn

When the school day ends, I'm more tired than I thought I would be. The bell ringing causes me to jump in my seat and I realize that I was just about to doze off. Honestly, the fact that I managed an hour of Professor Nightingale calling Draoich an abomination is a damn miracle. I'm surprised I never fell asleep the instant he started prattling on about how we started the Silva War, when we didn't.

So far, Magical Studies doesn't seem like my kind of jam.

I pack my books into the small feather bag Alice loaned me. Chairs screech across the rustic wooden floor as students prepare to leave. The only person I recognized in my last two classes was Gideon, who very generously spent the vast majority of them attempting to glare a hole into the back of my head.

Exhausted, I sling the bag over my shoulder, grab my cloak and leave the stuffy little classroom. I merge into the crowd of students buzzing through the hallways. Sirena and Alice don't seem to be around, but I catch a glimpse of Jasper, Alice's rabbit, darting around the corner.

Curious, I weave my way through the students and rush after him. He hops down another hallway and disappears into a small passage. I follow him as quickly as I can, only to discover that the passage leads to a set of spiral stairs. They're steep, just like every other staircase in this castle, and it feels like I've walked down a thousand of them by the time I reach the bottom.

Sunlight bleeds into my eyes. I take another step and emerge into a beautiful courtyard filled with the most gorgeous flowers I've ever seen. Hibiscus and primrose flutter around me. Rose bushes and bluebells line the cobbled pathway twisting around the freshly mown grass. There's countless species of flowers I don't recognise, but their brightly-colored petals are no less beautiful.

I seem to be alone. *Seem* to be. I know Jasper is hiding in here somewhere.

"Jasper?" I call out to him, peering into the nearest rosebush. Nothing. "Where are you, you little shit?"

He hops out of the rose bush and then darts through the flowerbeds, looking back to see if I'm following. I'm almost tempted to chase him if I wasn't so tired.

"You brought me here to play with you?" I shake my head at him. "What a strange little familiar you are."

Jasper stops to scratch an itch on his ear and I take another look around, wondering what on earth he brought me here for. It's clear that someone has poured a lot of love into this garden. Aside from the flowers and perfectly maintained grounds, there's also a greenhouse at the other end of the garden.

Jasper hops off again, scampering toward the greenhouse. I take a step after him, but a strange hand touches my right arm and I nearly jump out of my skin.

I instinctively raise my hands and gather a fireball. The

flames are light blue instead of dark green. I wonder how powerful this white magic will be?

Spinning around, I glare at the stranger who touched me. The young man is small and bent with a slightly haggard appearance. His auburn hair is unruly, curtaining half of his pale face. The only eye visible is blue and clearly too big for its socket. When he sees the fireball in my hand, he stumbles backward and frantically holds out his arms in supplication.

"You scared the hell out of me," I say, keeping the fireball visible until I know it's safe. "Who are you?"

The man moves his hands around in rapid motions, signalling that he's deaf. I glance down his clothes and realize that he's wearing a brown jumpsuit instead of a uniform. He's a member of staff.

I extinguish the fireball into my palm, then sign to him. ::Are you deaf?::

He seems surprised by my communication and pauses for a moment. ::You can also sign?::

I nod at him. ::My grandma was deaf.::

His beady eye widens in amazement. ::I'm sorry I gave you a fright. I didn't mean to.::

"It's okay," I reply, wondering if he can hear since he never really answered my question. "Can you hear me all right or is it easier if I signed?"

::I can still hear,:: he signs back, ::I'm just not able to speak.::

"What happened, if you don't mind me asking?"

Instead of replying, he points over my shoulder. I watch him step around me toward the greenhouse. That's when I notice he has a terrible limp and a hump on his left shoulder, forcing him to lean forward.

Out of nowhere, a goat appears and skips after the

man. Jasper seems to recognize the creature and runs circles around him. Curiosity always gets the better of me. I barely last one minute before I'm standing in the doorway of the greenhouse.

I've seen greenhouses before. This one is like a mansion. I have never seen such intricate glass-work in my life. It's almost like we're inside a gem instead of a building made for keeping plants warm. It's larger on the inside than I thought it would be and it occurs to me that the discrepancy is because the place is magical.

Well, duh. Of course it is.

There are wooden workbenches against the walls and a pair of aisles surrounded by cuttings and seedlings and delicate baby plants. Some of them are flowering and some are vegetables or fruits.

At the end of the greenhouse, inset in a circle of black glass up near the peak of the roof, is a breathtaking stained glass portrait. When I see who the portrait is of, my heart drops into my stomach. It's Esmeralda, my three-times great-grandmother. But she's young, much younger than she was when she was captured by Witch Hunters. Her long dark hair cascades over her shoulders in soft waves, her eyes are the same dark brown as my own and she's holding a baby goat in her arms. The same goat that had run past me not a moment ago.

I can't believe what I'm seeing. What is a portrait of my ancestor doing in here?

She's dressed just like every picture I've ever seen of her, in a beautiful off-the-shoulder white blouse, with big gold earrings and a colorful scarf around her head.

"This is why Jasper brought me here," I whisper to myself. Turning around, I sign, ::When was this window created?::

He pauses, looking back up at the glass. ::Around ten years ago. She was a professor here until...:: He stops, averting his gaze to the floor.

Until what, I want to ask, but I can see that he's uncomfortable with the subject. He might not want to share personal information with someone he's just met.

I look up at the portrait. This was made ten years ago? That would suggest my ancestor was still alive when Mom gave birth. Our mom died shortly after the delivery, so Grandma raised us. All she told me about Esmeralda was that she was taken from Draoich after giving birth to my grandfather. Now it turns out that she may have been alive all this time. She must be over one hundred and fifty years old.

My head spins with the information. Sure, witches age slowly once they reach full maturity. But if this is all true, why was Esmeralda, a Darkblood, teaching at Everafter Academy? And what happened to her? Why would she just abandon her family like that? Was she still part of the coven?

I'm not sure this guy is the person to ask about her, at least not right now. So I say instead, "This place is beautiful."

And it really is. I'm surprised I think so, since there's no black anywhere in the room.

My companion gestures to the stained glass. ::This is Esmeralda's Garden. It's a sacred place.::

"Sacred? And here I was trespassing," I groan, face-palming. "I'm sorry. I was chasing my friend's familiar and he came in here. I never knew this courtyard was private."

He shakes his hands. ::No, no. It's okay. I know Jasper. He's the rabbit, right?::

"Yeah, that's the guy."

::He's very talkative.::

I snort at that. "That's one way to describe him. Pain in the ass, more like."

The window catches my attention again. "What's your name? I just realized I never asked it. You know, before I almost toasted your ass."

He breathes a laugh through his nose and shakes his head. ::It's Quasimodo. Or Quasi.::

"That's a nice name." I smile and hold out my hand. "I'm Red."

Quasimodo looks up and stares at me for a moment. It's like he's trying to suss out if I'm genuine or not. Of course, I'm completely genuine. There's something truly sweet about Quasimodo. Maybe it's the way his smile lights up his face like sunbeams. He seems like he'll be a nice friend to have on my side.

Tentatively, he places a deformed hand into my own and we shake hands. I get the feeling he isn't used to people being willing to touch him.

At that moment, Jasper runs out of the greenhouse, chased by the goat.

I let go of Quasiomodo's hand and scramble the rabbit into my arms before he can escape. If Jasper brought me here to find out about Esmerelda and make a friend, I'm thankful. But if I find out it was just so he could have a playdate with a goat, I'm going to be pissed.

"It's time to get you back home," I tell Jasper, waving at Quasimodo with my free hand. "See you around, Quasi."

He waves at me, then finishes with, ::Take care of yourself.::

When I get back to the dorm room with Jasper, Broin is hopping along the headboard of my bed, the avian equivalent of pacing. He flaps his wings and squawks when he sees me.

I put Jasper in his cage, then turn to face him. "What's the matter now?"

—*You picking fights is what's wrong,*—he chides. —*Alice told me about it. She said it was awesome.*—

"It was."

—*It wasn't. It was a serious error and you need to be corrected. You're supposed to be blending in, not making sure you have an engraved entry on the headmaster's shit list.*—

I sigh with resignation. "I know. I'm sorry. I just... I got so mad, and..."

—*Jasper is listening. We can't talk in the open anymore.*—

I nod and sit down on my bed. He takes a short flight over to me so he can sit on my knee. I stroke his feathers, and we continue to talk.

—*It's so hard to be here. Every time I look at the place - this bed, these pillows, this class schedule - I just keep thinking that my sister is supposed to be here. I miss them so much.*—

—*I miss them, too. Big Red would want you to enjoy this experience, though. She'd want you to learn everything you can, make friends... and you know Grandma El would want you to avenge her.*— He looks at me with his dark, intelligent eyes. —*And you can't do that if you get expelled.*—

—*I promise I'll start blending in better.*— I sigh, knowing he's completely right. I never have been able to control my temper. That's got to change from now on. The last thing I want to do is get kicked out. Everything depends on me staying here.

I look out the window. The shadows are lengthening, and the sky is painted orange and pink like rainbow sherbet. Even the sky is prettier in this part of the forest. It's jarring.

Turning to Broin again, I say, —*I want to start hunting as soon as possible. Tonight, even. I think I should start where the wolves attacked at the Black Ravine and then track them from there.*—

—*See where they came from, or see where they went afterwards?*— Broin asks.

—*Both, if there's time. And you wouldn't believe what I saw today.*— I nod at Jasper, who is apparently focused on eating his bowl of carrots. —*I was chasing after his fuzzy little ass. And I found a portrait of Esmeralda - in a greenhouse. There was a man there and he told me it was made only ten years ago. How can that be possible? Grandma said Esmeralda was taken after giving birth to her son. How could she still be alive when I was nine years old?*—

Broin's silence speaks volumes.

—*You know something, don't you?*— I press him.

—*I know there was a rumour Esmeralda was still alive. That's why your grandfather left the coven. He went to find her, but he was never heard from again. Neither his nor Esmeralda's bodies were found.*—

I worry my bottom lip, chewing on his words. —*We need to find out more. If she really was a professor here, I'm sure other members of staff will remember her.*—

There's a reason Jasper took me into the courtyard today. I just need to figure out what.

The door opens, interrupting our conversation. Sirena and Alice come in and Alice is carrying a wicker picnic basket. She holds it up.

"Look! I found it in the library. Shouldn't Red Riding Hood have a basket?"

She puts it on the ground at my feet and I stare at it. "What am I supposed to carry in there?"

"Broin, maybe?" Sirena jokes. Broin doesn't think it's funny and gives her a tongue lashing, which to her is just a bunch of squawks.

Alice laughs, shrugging. "Books. Or herbs."

The look she gives me is pointed.

Sirena giggles and wiggles her eyebrows mischievously. "Or whiskey."

"Yeah, I don't think there's any of that around here," I say, smiling.

I pick up the basket. It's surprisingly sturdy, and it's got a false bottom lined with black cloth. I look up at Alice, who just smiles.

"You might think there's no booze around," Sirena says, winking at me. "But you'd be wrong."

I raise an eyebrow. "How so?"

They look at each other, then Alice says, "Follow us."

They take me on a circuitous path, first down one corridor, then another and finally into a maintenance closet.

I balk at the door. "I don't want to go back into the broom closet. I mean, I'm Out, you know?"

Sirena laughs, grabbing a candle from a wall sconce. "Just get in there."

We go in. Alice shoves aside a stack of cleaning supplies and exposes a stone wall. The mortar is discolored around a fairly large section of bricks and she shimmies those bricks out of the way. Once they start to move, I realize that it's really a door painted to look like bricks and englamoured to keep anyone from thinking twice. That's the thing about glamours - they only last until something breaks the illusion.

She opens the door and steps through, and I follow. Sirena brings up the rear, her flickering candle offering the only light. I remember wondering where Daddy Broin and I could get some alone time. I think I just found the spot.

The false door leads into a hallway that's about as long as a coach, but narrower. At the other end, I can see another door which Alice pushes open. Fresh air rushes in, blowing out Sirena's candle, but we don't really need it anymore. I can see the light from numerous torches burning in iron holders set into the building's stone crenellations.

"This is a maintenance access route," Alice tells me. "They come up here to do roof repairs when necessary and when simple magic from the ground doesn't fix whatever's broken."

"Which means," Sirena alludes, "that they hardly ever come up here. Alice dreamed about it and that's how we found it. And because I'm awesome, that's how we found this."

She opens another false door in the wall and reveals a wooden box filled with ice. Magic shimmers around the box, traces of an elemental cold spell. In the box is six pack of local ale.

"You've got booze?"

Sirena shrugs nonchalantly. "What kind of girls would we be if we didn't break the rules?"

"Oh, I don't know. Students of the year?" I offer, laughing. Sirena hands me a frosted beer. "I'm beginning to think you guys belong in Nevermore."

"I have a cousin who goes there," Alice chimes in, her

expression vacant as if she's getting a vision of some kind. "She says it's wonderful."

"Pssht, yeah, whatever," Sirena snorts. "I heard at least three students die every year of *natural causes*. Please. We all know that school's a cesspit."

Her words sting more than they should. It's not like I'm at that school or I'm even associated with it...anymore. But it's the judginess that gripes me. People are always quick to assume the worst of those they don't understand.

"I think there's two sides to every story," I counter, taking a swig of beer. The slightly bitter taste cools the back of my throat. I'm not a big drinker, but this tastes surprisingly good.

Alice nods slowly. "I do, too. You're too cynical."

Sirena guffaws and leans forward. "*Me,* cynical? That's rich coming from Miss Alice Underland who..." A quick glance at me suddenly stops whatever she was about to say. "Anyway, I just feel sorry for them sometimes. It's not their fault they were born into that kingdom."

"Here, here." I lift my beer and smile at them. "To the students at Nevermore Academy."

"Those unlucky bastards," Sirena adds and we clink bottles.

We settle down with our drinks and I look out over the view. This is the perfect vantage point to watch everything in this place. I can see the courtyard, the stable, the library and cafeteria. There are thick walls all around Everafter and multiple gates that give access in all four cardinal directions. One of the gates is right outside the dormitory and it conveniently opens into the forest. The school is surprisingly small and self-contained on the outside yet huge on the inside; the architecture on the inside doesn't seem to match the building that you see from the gate.

Also, the school looks different from the west gate than it does from the forest gate and the whole thing seems like an entirely different complex from the front.

Magic.

I'm about to mention this when a group of male students burst into view in the field beyond the wall, playing a spirited game of Flick. The game seems pretty stupid to me, but it involves a ball that's propelled around the field using specially-enchanted wands. There are nets on opposite sides of the field and the idea is to get the ball into the net using this magical propulsion. When one team is pushing toward the net, the other team is trying to push the ball away with their own wands. Sometimes the guys shoot each other, which is the only fun part of watching this game. They're laughing their asses off, which is sort of a shame, because there is some prime meat out there. They're all wearing tight white shorts and t-shirts.

Sirena smiles. "I'll be the first to say it. You can't deny they're snooties with voluptuous booties."

I gawp at her. "Did you just…?"

"Yes. Yes I did." She nods proudly, dusting off her shoulders. "And I'm not the only one. Everyone here calls them the Prince Charmings."

"Okay, but I'll remind you that Gideon is also a jerk," Alice points out. She adds in a mumble, "Not to mention Erik."

Sirena glares at her. "Yeah, but that doesn't mean we can't admire what the Storyteller gave them. As for Erik…" She sighs dreamily, watching him run in his tight white shorts. "It's complicated."

Alice rolls her eyes and whispers at me behind her hand. "Complicated? You mean it's catastrophic."

I have to agree with her. There's not a single person in

this school, apart from Broin, who I plan on getting to know intimately. I'm only here to find the Big Bad Wolf and his pack of Witch Hunters. I don't have time to date guys, or princes, or whatever the heaven Lucifer wants to throw my way.

For now, watching will be enough. I drink my beer and watch the princes play their game. Some day, I'm going to punch that Gideon in the throat.

Chapter Ten

Broin

The wind blows through my feathers as I soar over the treetops. The forest is blanketed in darkness, with only periodic candlelight bleeding through leaves. It's a beautiful Witching Hour and as much as I love my girl, I'm fucking relieved to be out of that castle.

How in the name of Lilith I'm going to survive being a familiar all day is beyond me. The thought of being trapped in a cage is enough to send me flying for the hills. But if spending most of my time cooped up is the only way to protect Ravyn, I'll do it and it will be the most beautiful cage in existence. It's the least I can do for her.

In four years' time, she'll be taken from me. I'm not even sure if I'll be able to go with her. I need to cherish every single moment until then. Her heart may belong to me, but her soul has been claimed by the Dark Lord and no fire on earth will erase that fact.

I was there last night, watching, waiting, hoping for an alternative solution. But there was none. While a barrier had been placed around the altar, I was still able to keep in contact through my bond with Ravyn. I felt her pain, just like I felt her pleasure and I knew that she was being saved as well as taken from me.

The Dark Lord has staked claim to her. He'll return once Ravyn graduates, seeking his payment in full and there's nothing I can do about that. The sigil carved into her flesh is eternal proof of that.

'Is it beautiful?'

It's fucking heartwrenching, I wanted to say, but she was so deliriously happy that I didn't want to take that away from her. She just lost her family, and possibly her coven for trying to leave. The last thing my girl needed was another disappointment.

My girl? Is she even my girl anymore? With so many potential mates at this academy, I'm not sure how much longer she'll allow me to be her Daddy, or even her protector.

A tinge of resentment creeps into me. I swoop through the trees, the smell of wildflowers invading my senses. I'm close to Lake Annan. The floral scents, burning my eyes, are a means of protection against evil spirits like me, but I have no choice but to fly through the trees and over the water to reach the other side. What looks like an ordinary pier stretching onto the surface is actually a hidden entrance to Poseida.

When I fly over the lake, the Citadel shines like a beacon in the distance. The High Council gather there to create bullshit laws, and most of the time, a war doesn't break out in the meantime. I've never cared much for the five members. I suppose my dislike grew when they tried to hang me for not dying the first time around.

The day Maxim Hemlock saved my life, I vowed to protect his family, down to the last one. I never thought that day would actually come—when only one Hemlock would be alive.

My mood sours at the thought. I was a piss-poor soldier, brother and son. Now I'm a failure at being a knight for those I love.

Well, hopefully tonight I can redeem that a little.

After two hours of endless rivers and trees, the Black Ravine swells into sight. The exact location of Rosso Lupa is unknown but the caves here have become a popular hideout for them over recent years. Fortunately, the ground seems to be spared of them for now. I'm almost tempted to shift and hunt these fuckers down on foot, but a raven is less conspicuous.

I hop and fly between the trees, looking for tracks. The tree where Ravyn had been cornered and stabbed remains smeared in her blood. In my raven form, blood glows, and Ravyn's is green like our lord's flame. The large patches of gold are from the hunters and one of the blood trails leads toward the cave.

There's nothing inside apart from bats, who aren't happy about me disturbing them. Going by the amount of blood that's in here, the hunters must have dragged their dead into the cave to hide them from predators.

I scour the surrounding area for more blood. Praise Satan, I find droplets that lead me out of the ravine. The hunters were badly injured when they left here. Fucking serves them right. I'm heading east now, toward Ravyn's home, and I really hope I'm about to find the hunters' bodies along the way.

I don't. Their blood and scents lead me past Ravyn's home, but then they disappear. All I have to track now are their scents, which are mixed with the rest of the pack that killed El and Redera.

Fury surges through me when I fly over the decimated remains of Hemlock Cottage. To have gone like that at the hands of Rosso Lupa mutts... It's incomprehensible. They were already hanging from the tree by the time I arrived the first time. When Ravyn let me take down their bodies, I used magic to remove the nails from their hands and feet. I didn't want Ravyn to suffer more than she had already.

If only I hadn't gone hunting that night. Maybe they would still be alive. Maybe I could have convinced Ravyn not to go to the altar. It's not her fault this happened. If anyone's to blame, it's me. I had avoided talking about the subject, hoping she'd drop it; instead it only made things worse. How I fucking wish I'd known Lucifer would have no choice but to revoke his protection. None of this might ever have happened.

I'm lost in my bitter thoughts and following the scent on autopilot. When I find a safe place to land and look up, I'm back at Everafter Academy.

This can only mean one thing.

The Witch Hunters *are* hiding at the academy.

Ravyn was right.

I fly up to her bedroom window on the fourth level. It's still slightly open, and when I hop inside, Ravyn is asleep on top of the blankets. She's still wearing her school uniform.

Don't tell me you were waiting up for me, Little Red?

Smiling for the first time today, I jump onto the floor and shift into my human form. I know it's risky, but I can't help myself and the other girls are asleep too; the ale I left for Alice to find in the maintenance closet made sure of that.

I press my lips to Ravyn's forehead. She stirs but

doesn't wake, so I trail my lips down to her mouth and kiss her, my hand itching to caress her beautiful face. It's been so long since I've had fun with her, I almost want to keep kissing her and touching her body.

With tremendous effort, I choose to ease her under the covers and shift back into a raven. I nestle into her neck and drape my wing protectively over her shoulder. *If could take your pain away, Little Red, I'd do it in a heartbeat.*

Chapter Eleven

Ravyn

In the morning, my roomies and I go to the cafeteria to get some breakfast. I'm not terribly enthused about the food here, so my expectations are low.

Yup. Just like I thought. The breakfast options aren't any better than lunch and dinner had been. At least they didn't boil everything this time.

I pick a croissant and a bowl of fresh fruit, the one thing the cooks couldn't ruin, and I join Alice and Sirena at the table. I pass the Princess Posse and they glare daggers at me, hoping I'll burst into flames. I smile and flip them off, receiving a trio of horrified gasps. Erik and Gideon are hanging out with them again, so at least all the assholes are in one place. I give them an extra finger and flip them off, too, but they just laugh.

I sit down beside Alice and across from Sirena. "Looks like I'm officially the school outcast."

"Take it as a compliment," Alice shrugs. "People who can see and do things other people can't always get ostracized."

Sirena nods in agreement. "It's their loss. Keep letting your freak flag fly and ignore those catty bitches."

"I can do that." I grin at them. "It's easy to ignore things that don't matter."

We're almost done with our meal when Aurora and her three toadies get up to leave the cafeteria. They walk directly past our table and accidentally-but-totally-on-purpose bump into my back. The still-healing mark from Lucifer reminds me that it's there, despite my magic trying to heal it. I hiss in surprise at the sudden pain and Alice looks at me in concern. I glare over my shoulder at Gideon, the one who ran into me. One day, I'm going to beat him to death, I swear to Satan, and I'm going to laugh the whole fucking time.

"Oops," he says, grinning at me.

"Fuck you," I snarl back.

He clicks his tongue at me like a disappointed nanny and continues on his way out of the cafeteria with the rest of the asshole patrol.

"What a dick," Sirena grumbles, staring at Erik in particular.

"Yeah."

"Did he hurt you?" Alice asks, an almost sinister note in her usually soft voice.

I smile at them. "No. I was just surprised, that's all." It's mostly true, so I don't feel like I'm lying.

The bell rings and Sirena stands up. "Time for class, girls."

I pop the last grape into my mouth and follow her. Today's morning class is Enchantments with Professor Martha Huckleberry. As the name implies, she's fey, some kind of nymph or other. I'm not too good at identifying Seelie fey. I've got a lot more experience with the Unseelie Court.

I sit down in one of the chair-desk combination seats

and look around. Aurora and Gideon are already here and there are a bunch of students I don't recognize. Christopher walks in and sits down in the desk beside mine.

"Hi."

What does he want?

I respond in a neutral tone. "Hi."

He looks away, almost as if he's shy. I don't completely buy this yet. Sure, he's not the meanest of the three, but Broin's right, I can't trust everyone here. He's probably trying to act all innocent so I do trust him, just so his friends can kick me in the teeth. *Not happening, dude.*

When class starts, Huckleberry doesn't waste time going over a syllabus or reinventing the wheel. Instead, she passes out spell books and wooden dolls.

"These dolls are the foci for your spells," she announces, her voice musical and pretty, because of course it is. "You will place all of your enchantments on these mannequins."

Poppets. No problem.

She gives me a strange look as she puts my book and doll down in front of me. "Miss Hemlock," she greets, arching one of her bushy eyebrows.

I smile back as sweetly as Redera would have. "Professor."

"You have... great power."

Aurora turns around in her seat and glares at me.

No kidding. Aloud, I say, "Uh... thanks?"

Professor Huckleberry finishes her rounds and goes back to the head of the class. "Turn to the first spell in your books."

I open the leather-bound cover and look at the first vellum page. The spell is more or less magical spray paint - it's just going to change the doll's color. I was casting this spell when I was four years old. I sigh, feeling stupid for hoping for more.

Aurora hears me and snips, "What's the matter? Too hard?"

Somehow I resist the urge to cast the spell on *her*. She'd look awesome in paisley. Maybe it'll be the next trend. *Hmm, it's tempting.*

"Too easy," I shoot back, giving a clearly false smile.

"Hmph." She turns back to face the front, flicking her wavy blonde hair over her petite shoulders. Beside her, Rapunzel gives me a withering look. It's getting tedious.

The professor continues. "In enchantment, as with all magic, words matter, but most of all, it's imagination that counts. Enchantment spells are limited only by what you believe. It's the one area of magic where faith in yourself and your abilities really comes into play."

I have to disagree with her. Summoning is the kind of magic where you have to believe in yourself the most just to be able to control whatever it is you pulled out of the ether. I guess Huckleberry isn't big on summoning, though, and I don't think it's even taught here at Everafter. I imagine it's more of a Nevermore thing, seeing as it forces whatever you summon into temporary slavery.

Whatever. It's not like it lasts forever. Besides, sometimes being a slave can be fun, if you have the right Master.

"Now, class." Huckleberry clears her throat. "Cast that first spell."

All around me, these rubes start sweating it, furrowing their brows and trying hard to do the thing. Aurora gets her poppet to change color pretty quickly, going from wood grain to pink.

Of course it would be pink.

I decide to make mine a little more interesting. While the other students lift their hands and mumble the words of the spell out loud, I cast from my mind, which is the only way to fly where enchantments are concerned. Think it and it will happen, Grandma always told me. So I think black background with silver stars that glow and twinkle, like the mannequin is made out of the night sky. It changes its appearance immediately. It's a parlor trick, but I'm pleased.

Next to me, Christopher breathes, "Wow..."

I look at his mannequin. It's a pleasant shade of green and I'm a little surprised by his choice of color. I suppose he chose the color of his eyes, the kind of green that looks almost blue.

Professor Huckleberry hurries over to me and seizes the poppet from my desk.

I'm convinced that I'm about to get in trouble when she holds it up to the class and shouts, "Everyone stop what you're doing and look at this magnificent creation!"

Everyone looks. Jaws drop. These idiots are so easily impressed.

"This is a masterful enchantment!" the professor announces. "And it illustrates what I was saying. Enchantment magics depend on your imagination. Don't be limited by what you think we want to see. Create the things *you* want to see."

She puts the doll back on my desk and beams at me. "I expect great things from you. I've never seen such mastery on the first day of class."

Gideon fake-coughs into his hand. "Darkblood."

A few of the students titter nervously and Huckleberry looks at him with disappointment on her face. "That's enough, Gideon. You know Darkblood witches aren't allowed here in Everafter. White witches, however, are rare and always welcome." She smiles at me, then continues to go from desk to desk.

Aurora is concentrating on her doll. She's probably trying to do something more interesting than matte pink. Her imagination is apparently very limited because she only manages pale yellow pinstripes.

No shock there.

The rest of class is a drag but not entirely painful. While the others try to master the simplest of simple spells, I keep changing the colors on my mannequin and read ahead in the book. It's the perks of being a witch; I already know most of the spells in it. There are some spells that I don't know, though, and that's a good sign. I might learn something in this joint after all.

Class breaks up, and we make our way out to the courtyard between classroom buildings. I recognize a familiar face and smile when I see Quasi trimming a swan-shaped ornamental topiary. I go over to him.

"Hey Quasi," I greet. "So, you're a groundskeeper?"

He looks around and then tucks the clippers under his arm so he can sign, ::You shouldn't be seen talking to me.::

"Why not?"

Quasi hesitates, then says, ::The other students won't like it if you talk to the help.::

"I don't care what the other students like." I lift my chin defiantly.

As if he's trying to prove me wrong, Gideon chooses that moment to stroll up to us. He's got a piece of paper in his hand and when he reaches us, he wads it up and drops it on the ground at Quasi's feet.

Gideon looks him in the eye. "Whoops. Guess you'd better pick that up."

Quasi bends to get the paper, but Gideon kicks the crumpled ball away. I can't take this fool another minute.

"Stop being an asshole," I snap at him.

He just laughs. "It figures that you'd be over here. I guess you found one of your own kind."

"What do you mean, my own kind?"

He looks at Quasi, then at me. "A Darkblood who doesn't belong here."

::I'm not Darkblood,:: Quasi signs, his face panicked.

Gideon laughs and mocks his sign language, waving his hands meaninglessly. I punch him in the shoulder, mostly because at the angle he's standing, his throat is just out of reach.

He looks at me in surprise. "You hit me!"

"Yeah and I'll do it again if you don't knock it off," I growl. "And I'll be aiming *much* lower this time. Although, it'll be hard to find it. Shall I fetch some tweezers?"

His face darkens with anger. He's so pathetic that I laugh. One little comment is all it takes to get him close to losing his temper. I wonder how it feels to be so fucking weak. I hate bullies. I hate spoiled princes. And one way or another, Gideon is going to get a taste of his own medicine. They all are. Even Redera wouldn't stand by while innocent people are being treated like muck.

He turns and stomps away like an infant.

Quasi turns to me with a sad little smile. ::You didn't have to do that.::

"Yes, I did. Assholes like him need to be brought down a peg or two."

He smiles a little wider and goes back to trimming the topiary. I get a weird urge to hug him, which is not like me at all. I walk away frowning. *Me? Hugging someone I barely know?*

I think I need to get laid.

The next class is double Familiar Handling. If they only knew all the ways I've handled Broin... I'm pretty sure that's not the sort of handling they mean. I go up to my room to retrieve him. I really hate that I have to keep him in my room all day. It seems abusive to me, and I wonder what's wrong with these white magic people if they're so afraid of familiars. Why the fuck have them, then?

He's sitting in his cage looking dejected when I go in. Jasper is already gone, so we're all alone. I open the door to Broin's cage and reach in to touch him.

—*Hi, Daddy.*—

He usually brightens up when I call him that, but today it seems like nothing's going to make him happy. I've never seen him so depressed. I wonder if he's been sitting grieving all day, and I feel guilty that I haven't been. Any time my emotions try to claw to the surface, I force them back down. My excuse is that I need to stay focused on the business of finding this wolf and fitting in here, but the truth? The truth is that I'm afraid that if I let myself start grieving I'll never be able to stop.

Broin hops onto my hand and I pull him free of his little prison. I stroke his feathers. "Sorry about this. I hate that I have to cage you."

—*I'm not a fan, myself.*— He turns his head away, looking anywhere but at me. —*Familiar Handling time?*—

"Yeah. Too bad you're not in your human form. We could teach them a thing or two about handling," I joke, desperately trying to jolly him out of his depression. He was gone all night, and when I woke up, he didn't speak all that much.

He makes a sound that's a cross between a click and a snort.

"What's the matter?"

Broin shifts his weight from one foot to the other, then admits, —*I'm losing you.*—

If I were the kind to tell white lies, I'd say something to make him feel better. But we both know the truth.

"In four years," I remind him softly. "Not right now."

—*What will I do if he doesn't let me follow you?*—

I sigh. This morose ruminating isn't like Broin at all. I think losing my family has hurt him as much as it's hurt me. He's just so good at hiding it. Is that why he left last night?

"You worship him, too. I don't see why he'd make you stay behind. Honestly, I don't know if you'd even want to come. He's going to make me his entertainment and I don't think that's something you'd want to see."

—*Maybe, if I'm there, I can mitigate things for you.*—

If he was in human form, I'd hug the stuffing out of him. For now, we have a stupid class to get to.

"Try not to think about it until you have to," I advise. "We have wolves to hunt and people to mess with. Let's just take each minute as it comes."

He flies up to sit on my shoulder and leans against my head, his chest against my ear. I can hear his heartbeat. It beats so fast when he's in bird form. I reach up and stroke his feathers, and he makes a contented trilling sound in the back of his throat.

—*I'll try,*— he says. —*No promises.*—

FAMILIAR HANDLING IS A FUCKING JOKE. IT'S ALL ABOUT how to call a familiar and how to bond with them. Seriously? If these yokels don't know that much, they don't deserve a familiar. It's a waste of a magical animal.

I'm irritated, so I tell the girls to eat lunch without me and I take Broin on a walk around campus. For the first time, I'm seeing other students with their familiars, too. It's refreshing to see all the animals, magical and ordinary alike, roaming the grounds freely. Just a pity they can't do that all day, every day.

A large, fluffy white dog runs up to me and plants its paws in the dirt, stiff-legged. I know canines well enough to know that it's not feeling friendly. A black cat follows, its tail lashing the air as it approaches, hackles up and giving a low growl.

I look around for the students these familiars are attached to. I'm not at all surprised to see Princess Pisspot and her Poser Posse coming my way. Aurora, Cinder and Rapunzel march up, followed by Gideon and Erik. The other one, Christopher, is absent from the gang.

Broin sends an aggressive caw in their direction, casting aspersions on their family lines. A sparrow lands on Rapunzel's shoulder and whistles back.

Great. What now?

Aurora gets right up in my personal space. "I don't like you."

"Really? I had no idea," I counter dryly.

"None of us like you. In fact, you're not welcome here at Everafter. We don't like witches." She has the temerity to jab me in the chest with her manicured finger. "You need to leave before things get a whole lot nastier."

I want to grab her finger and break it off. It's getting harder and harder to act like my sister. I'm just not that nice. When I see shitty people do shitty things, something inside me snaps, especially when they're claiming to be a good person. At least villains own our darkness. It's a part of who we are and we don't try to hide that. Fake people like this prefer to stab others in the back so they can bathe in their blood. I despise that sort of fakeness, and it's exactly why I've been dishing out as much as these snobs keep giving me.

—*Don't stoop to their level. You're better than that, Little Red.*—

Broin's right, of course, but I'm seriously starting to lose my shit.

I jab Aurora's chest the same way she just jabbed mine. "You don't own this school. Stop acting like you do and just leave me alone. Don't you have anything better to do with your time?"

She tosses her hair and narrows her eyes into little green slits. "I'll have you know that my mother is the queen of Talia and we are the richest kingdom in our world. I own everything... and everybody. If you touch me again, I will have you hanged."

That's it. I fucking lose it.

—*Ravyn, don't!*—Broin shouts through our bond, but my anger erupts and all I see is red. Before I can stop myself, I haul off and slap the bitch across her pretty little face. She almost falls from the impact. Gideon catches her before she hits the ground, which by my way of thinking is unfortunate. I would have loved to see her face plant.

Rapunzel starts shrieking. "Who do you think you are? How *dare* you, a measly witch of all people, lay a hand on a princess?!"

Cinder claps her gloved hands together and speaks in a high-pitched tone. "Oh, things are getting interesting!"

Erik puts a hand on Rapunzel's shoulder, holding her back. He looks at me with utter disdain. "I heard what you did in Enchantments class. I don't know how you got into Everafter, but you're evil, and you belong in Nevermore. I'm gonna send you back there one way or another."

I plant my feet, ready to fight it out. "You're all welcome to try."

"Witch!" Rapunzel yells. "Darkblood! You *should* be hanged!"

My anger explodes into white-hot fury as images of Grandma and Redera invade my mind. The tree. The nooses. The fire. My heart's racing so fast I can barely breathe.

"You're so upset about my enchantments?" I pull my lips into a superficially calm smile. "Try this one on for size."

I whisper the words of power and feel the dark energy rising in the depths of my being. It fills my chest, my arms, my fingers, and then Rapunzel's blonde hair unravels from its braid. The locks turn into snakes. She screams in terror, frozen to the spot, her eyes wide with fear. It's a beautiful thing and it only gets better.

She starts swatting at her head, running in circles like a raving lunatic. Her hair actually *bites* her! One of the snake heads in her new Medusa hairdo latches onto her cheek and sinks its teeth in.

Rapunzel wails and I can't stop laughing, despite the fact that I've pretty much showed everyone here that I know dark magic. That doesn't mean I'm a Darkblood, though, at least not to them. I'd have to do something way darker than a silly prank to convince them of that.

Aurora tries to counterspell, but she just manages to turn the snakes pink, which is really adding insult to injury. Erik backs away, completely useless, and the dog starts barking its head off. Gideon grabs its collar and holds it back. I guess I know where the dog belongs now.

A shrill whistle blows.

Mrs. Thornhart runs into view. "Stop!" she commands, looking equal parts terrified and aggrieved. "Turn her back this instant!"

Reluctantly, I flick my hand and remove the spell. Rapunzel's hair stops writhing and turns back into her usual locks. Funny enough, when I removed the spell, it stripped away all of the spells she had - and turns out miss golden hair isn't so golden without her dye job. Who knew? I'm surprised it wasn't a wig.

Mrs. Thornhart is shaking her whistle at me. "This is unacceptable! Headmaster Lockwood has very strict rules about the misuse and abuse of magic! And he saw you."

She points at a circular window high up in the side of the tallest of the school's round towers. I can see a shape that might be Professor Lockwood standing there, staring down at us.

Broin sighs, shaking his little head. —*Good one, Ravyn. Way to fuck things up again on your second day.*—

Chapter Twelve

Ravyn

Fucking things up doesn't even come close to describing my day.

—*I'm sorry I disappointed you,*— I tell Broin as I follow Mrs. Thornhart through the castle. She stalks past the Great Hall and down a long winding hallway. Her intense speed-walking makes it seem like she's trying to outrun me. —*But I'm not sorry for teaching that bitch - them all - a lesson. It had to be done. They were even bullying Quasi!*—

—*But look where it's got you. Don't you see? Small actions like a minor hex can have major consequences.*—

—*Are you going to punish me later?*—

He pauses for a moment. I hurry after Thornhart up a set of spiral stairs. The sunlight pouring through the windows cause prisms to dance around me. It's like I'm trapped in a kaleidoscope.

—*You know I have to. Your recklessness is getting out of hand again. I let your tone slide earlier, but today could be enough to get you expelled.*—

I sigh, but I won't lie when I say a part of me quivers with excitement.

Hopefully we'll be able to use the maintenance closet

for a couple of hours. I haven't been punished in nearly a week and the tension in my body craves release. Even then, Broin had gone easy on me that day for hexing Redera. It wasn't my fault she was being so annoying and kept messing up all my potions.

Another sigh leaves me, this time heavy with despair.

I'd give anything to fight with my twin again. To hear her laugh, practice magic with her, make potions at midnight while Grandma makes our favorite witches' brew.

A crushing weight presses on my heart, dragging me back down to reality again. I frown at the never-ending stairs. By the time I reach the top of them, I'm out of breath and have to lean against the wall. Mrs. Thornhart turns her steely eyes on me and I straighten up with a smile. With a slow shake of her head, she knocks on a set of doors. They're at least eight feet tall with gold leaves embellished in the wood.

"Come in."

Mrs. Thornhart ushers me into Lockwood's office and leaves as quickly as she can. The inside of the tower is even more beautiful than its exterior. There's elaborate woodwork and bookcases filled with leather-bound tomes. A rolling ladder runs on a track that goes all around the room and the furniture is a dark heavy wood created with an eye for detail. The desk is carved with an intricate pattern of vines, leaves and flowers that shimmer in the light pouring through the glass ceiling.

Professor Lockwood is standing at the window facing away from me, his hands clasped behind his back. For a breathless moment, I think he has a cane in his hand, but it's just a trick of the light. When I realize he's not holding anything, I don't know if I'm disappointed or relieved.

"I watched that little performance," he begins, his voice gravelly with displeasure. He doesn't even turn around. "Would you care to explain yourself?"

Not really.

Broin shifts on my shoulder and I think he's getting ready to peck Lockwood's eyes out if he has to. The eagle perched on a gold stand by his desk trains his eyes on me, his red eyes unblinking.

"Aurora was suggesting that I be hanged," I answer, holding my head up high. "I couldn't just stand by and let that slide when so many of my kind have suffered that fate."

He turns to face me, and his eyes are *burning*.

There's serious anger in there—a darkness I didn't expect. He stalks around his desk and it occurs to me that he's fucking huge. Bigger than Broin, and that's saying something. He backs me right up against the door and stands just a few inches away, so close his hot breath fans my cheeks.

"If something like that happens again, you are to notify Mrs. Thornhart at once. She is assigned to your year for a reason."

When he stands this close, I can feel power crackling through him. He's no ordinary man. Just from our proximity, the hairs on my body stand on end as if I've stepped into the Devil's Altar. He stares into my eyes, his bowed lips pressed in a firm line. The pressure of his power and darkness reaches into me and snakes around my heart, whispering sweet evils. My mouth falls open though I don't make a sound.

Who the heaven is this man? Or rather, *what* is he?

"Yes, what Miss Briar said was out of line and she will be reprimanded. But this is the second transgression today,

Miss Hemlock. Are you setting out to break all of the rules on purpose or does it just come naturally to you?"

He steps away and turns his back on me again.

"Witches are rarely tolerated here at Everafter, and if they are, it's because they are *white* witches. You and I both know the spell you just cast comes from a dark source." His large hands grip each other and I'm grateful my neck isn't between them. "If you ever cast dark magic like that again on academy grounds, you will be expelled. If I ever see you casting *any* magic outside of your studies, I will have no choice but to enact discipline."

I must be recovering my wits, because that sounds really fucking promising.

"Now return your familiar to its cage and go to your next class."

Stunned, I turn toward the door. That went...surprisingly easy. I'm a little disappointed. There's darkness lurking in the headmaster and I want to break it out.

I stop and look back at him, figuring today's the day to press my luck. "Why must our familiars to be kept in cages? Isn't that barbaric?"

"This is a school, Miss Hemlock, not a zoo." He pauses and turns around, the muscles working hard along his clenched jaw. "It's not something I have control over, nor is it something you should concern yourself with."

Of course Professor Lockwood doesn't control the laws here.

The High Council do.

At least our government, Maleficis Invictus, actually know how to treat our familiars as equals.

"What about an arena?" I ask casually, recalling how I'd once been to an arena. They take up little space on the outside, but the interior is enough to hold a million football pitches. Sort of like this castle. "I'm not sure if it'll work, but isn't it worth a shot? I'm sure they'd be grateful to run around during the day."

And escape the students who clearly don't know how to handle them.

His slate-blue eyes flash. "I told you, Miss Hemlock. I do not make this rule and I will not repeat myself again." His body is rigid, telling me he's barely keeping his anger in check. "You are dismissed."

I incline my head and leave his office.

Outside, Broin remarks, —*That went well.*—

—*I just hate the thought of you being in a cage all day,*— I reply, climbing down the stairs. —*It's not fair.*—

—*It's the rules. You need to follow them.*—

"When have I ever been good at following rules?" I snort, saying the words out loud.

"Miss Hemlock." Professor Lockwood's voice catches me off guard and I let out a yelp. "How long does it take to walk down these stairs?" He sweeps by me and climbs down them, adding without so much as a backward glance, "My rules are ones you *will* be following at my academy."

I just manage to stop myself asking, 'Is that a threat or a promise, Sir?', but Broin squeezes my shoulder. I bite back the retort and continue walking two steps behind.

Walking behind Professor Lockwood, in utter silence? Yeah. This is definitely going up there with the most awkward moments in my life. But damn, does he smell good. I take this moment to look over his body, and his ass is even better than his musk.

His navy suit is tailored perfectly around his huge, muscular body, framing his ass like a ripe peach. Damn if I don't want to sink my teeth into it. When he looks over at me, I give him my sweetest of smiles. He ignores me and turns back, but that's when I see something interesting.

The tip of a tattoo below the nape of his neck.

Beard, tattoos, and a sinister air about him? There's definitely more to this headmaster than meets the eye, and I'm the girl to find out what that is.

We go separate ways at the bottom of the stairs. Watching Professor Lockwood stalk down the hallway, I can't help but feel intrigued by him. There's something menacing that calls out to me, mirroring my own dark heart.

Broin senses it too, because he stays silent all the way back to my room. When I step inside, Sirena is bent down to place Jasper into his cage.

"Hey, where's Alice?" Broin flies off my shoulder and into his cage. I don't bother actually locking it so that, when Broin knows it's safe, he can wander freely.

Sirena closes Jasper's cage and smiles at me. "She's at the infirmary."

An unexpected fear grips me. "Why? Is she okay?"

"Oh, yeah. She just gets really bad episodes sometimes."

"Episodes?"

"Headaches. Fits. Extreme fatigue."

I sit down on my bed, thinking about sweet Alice in the infirmary. She said her power exhausts her because it keeps her awake when the rest of the world is asleep. Does it do more than that? She always looks drained whenever I see her.

"Is there anything we can do to help?" I pick my bag up and sling it over my shoulder. "Maybe we can make a healing potion or something."

Spinning around, Sirena shakes her head while tucking

Augustus under her shirt. "I've known her since we were, like, six or seven? She started having these seizures when we were around eight. She just sort of changed then, but she usually bounces back after a few hours."

That's a relief. I never expected to care so much about these girls, but I do.

"Where's Alice from?" Sirena gives me a stupid look and I quickly realize my mistake. "Oh, sweet fuck. Her name. Underland. Is that where she's from?" She nods. "Well, shit."

That means she's from Draoich like me.

Sirena grabs her pink satchel and nods. "Told you we all have secrets. That's how Alice knew you were a Darkblood."

Walking out of the door, I'm still intrigued to know how a Draoich and Poseidan became friends. Those kingdoms aren't exactly friendly neighbours.

"So how did you guys meet?"

Before Sirena answers, Broin speaks in my mind. — *After class, you'll come back here and tell your roommates we're going for a walk. Remember your knife.*—

I swallow. Hard. He's in Daddy Mode and I fucking love it.

We walk down the stairs and through the emptying common room. Double Defence Training with Professor Mulan is going to take up the afternoon, which I'm actually looking forward to. Kicking more butt today sounds like a great way to let off some steam. We head toward the ground floor to meet the class in the dojo.

"I met Alice when I was six," Sirena finally answers. "My dad divorced my mum then and I was pretty cut up about it. God, the whole kingdom was." She shakes her head and I glimpse tears in her eyes. "Anyway, I ended up swimming away and falling through a portal. Next thing I know, I'm caught in a fishing net on the coast of Neverland. Alice helped me escape before any of the Lost Boys found me." Entering the main courtyard, she adds with a wink, "I've been trying to get rid of her ever since but she just sticks to you like seaweed."

I burst out laughing, my side twitching from the impact. "You know something, I'm so fucking glad we all became friends."

Sirena links her arm with mine. "You and me both, sista. You and me both."

Chapter Thirteen

Ravyn

Professor Hua Mulan is a force to be reckoned with. Before introductions are made, we're told to run ten laps around the biggest field I've ever seen and this is only the warm-up.

Luckily I'm good at running. I've spent my whole life running away from Witch Hunters and healthy cuisine. So it's pretty much the best non-magical skill I have.

Some of the other students aren't as fast on their feet, the poor little babies. The students who do lag are made to do extra laps while we get to watch from the sidelines. Watching Rapunzel sweat and heave like a pregnant nun is pure comedy gold. Looks like princesses aren't perfect at everything. As for her hair? The infirmary must have counteracted the hex. Such a pity.

I'm exhausted when class is over. It felt more like boot camp than anything. Running, push-ups, squats and anything else the professor could use to test our endurance. I actually respect her as a teacher though. She wants to whip these pretty boys and girls into shape and I'm living for it.

—*It's time for your punishment.*—

Broin's voice causes a shiver to run down my spine. Those words are like music to my ears.

After taking a drink from the water fountain, I wave at Sirena, who's busy giving Erik a well-deserved earful. For once I actually see him look a little hurt by her comments and he goes to follow her, but Gideon places a hand on his shoulder and pulls him away. It really pisses me off that Gideon looks sexy with his cheeks flushed and slightly damp hair. I'm not even going to mention the way he fills out his tight shorts.

Scowling, I turn away and enter the changing rooms. Sirena steps into the cubicle next to me. While we shower and get dressed, she talks about Erik and how she's tired of the way he treats her. I suggest she kick him in the nads, but she laughs and says he'd probably dodge that like he dodges his royal responsibilities.

His father is King Gareth of Aira, the kingdom at the north of the Great Forest. Just like his pretentious leather coat, Erik is all about playing the irresponsible jerk to win all the girls. He doesn't want to ascend the throne when he turns twenty-two. She doubts he even wants her.

"We're betrothed," she says as we step out of the changing rooms.

I come to a stop. "No. Fucking. Way."

"Way." She nods, rolling her eyes and snorting. "Since before we were born. But the worst part of all? I *do* like him. When it's just the two of us, he isn't such an asshole, you know?"

"He just puts up a front," I offer, knowing his type quite well.

For a short time I dated Damon Salvador, our coven's future High Priest. He was very similar. Grandma was so proud of our relationship but I grew tired eventually. The typical bad-guy persona bored me to heaven. The guy used to get me to kill his spiders, for hell's sake. That's not the kind I look for in mates.

I need real men—not boys.

"Do you want to hang out tonight?" Sirena asks over a yawn. "I don't know about you, but I'm beat. Maybe you can conjure some pizza and we can chill in our room?"

That does sound amazing, but I already have an...appointment.

"I'd love to but I'm going for a walk with Broin. It's so unfair that he needs to be caged all day."

A hand goes to her neck, where her necklace and familiar are hiding. "I can't even imagine. That's why..." Lowering her voice, she whispers, "I have this. Augustus doesn't only protect the locket. He's able to go through the portal when he feels like it."

"That's a relief. I was starting to wonder if you were trying to smother him with your breasts."

A scarlet tinge rises to her cheeks. "*No!* ... Gosh, I don't have much anyway."

I wrap an arm around her and rub her shoulders, surprising even myself. "You're a Queen who's going to be slaying this school, girl. Own it."

She laughs and we climb the stairs to our dormitory. Inside our room, I'm sad to see Alice still isn't around. I hope she's okay. Maybe I should try a potion just in case.

Broin is perched on top of his cage with my dagger beside him. I grin and slip it into my sock when Sirena isn't looking. Broin flies up to my shoulder, and after telling Sirena that I'll be back later, I close the door behind us.

Students swarm the hallways. I can hear them going wild in the common room, too. Not that it's really necessary, but I cast a glamour so we can walk through undisturbed.

"*Valamen.*" As I whisper the incantation and rotate my finger anti-clockwise, a nearly transparent veil drops around me. I hold my nose to suppress a sneeze. Glamours don't always work and a more powerful witch can easily detect them, which is why I don't use them often. Plus they make me sneeze and they're friggin' cold. I rub my arms against the icy chill settling over me.

—*Do you remember the maintenance closet?*— His tone is hard, adding to my shivers.

—*Yes.*—

—*I want you to go in there.*—

Even though it was dark, I remember the path the girls showed me before. I walk into the common room to make my escape. Just as I was expecting, Gideon is sitting near the fire, slouched in an armchair like it's his throne. Only Christopher is with him, though he's busy reading a book. I catch wind of their conversation and pause for a moment.

"The Darkblood has got to go," Gideon drawls, running a hand lazily through his short hair.

Christopher looks up from his book. "Why do you despise her so much? She's just a girl."

Gideon's face twists into an ugly grimace. "Because she's a *freak*. Because she's *contaminated*. Because we all fucking know that she doesn't belong here and *should* be hanged like the good old days." Raising his voice so that students look over at him, he shouts, "Because no Darkblood has ever been to this academy and they never will be."

His declaration receives a round of applause. Next

they'll be getting out pitchforks. A red-haired girl turns around in her seat to frown at him.

"How do you even know for sure that she's a Darkblood?"

"Because I do!" Gideon snaps, glaring venomously at her. That's really not much of an answer, but whatever.

Christopher sighs heavily and goes back to reading his book. The girl returns to her business, too. My blood boils through my veins. Half of me wants to hex Gideon, but Broin nudges me with his beak and I leave the common room without making a scene.

A contaminated freak who deserves to be hanged just for existing? And they say Draoichs are the villains. I'm beginning to think Everafter wouldn't be so different to Nevermore after all.

The closet isn't far once I leave the common room. Two corridors later, I'm standing outside the door, and my heart skips a beat. I wrap my hand around the handle, which is soaked in dark magic.

From the moment we step into the closet, our dynamic changes.

Broin shifts into his man, wearing just a pair of pants that hang loosely on his hips. His long hair is tousled over his broad shoulders and the dark look in his eyes sends a rush of desire through me. A part of me that gets locked up until moments like this crawls to the surface, free at last.

Gone is the defiant, rebellious Ravyn that takes no man's shit. Now I'm just a witch, standing in front of her Daddy, wishing he'd bend her over his knee already.

He reaches out and caresses the side of my face. "How I've missed touching you like this," he whispers, his nose brushing mine.

I close my eyes and lean into his touch. "I've missed it too, Daddy."

"It seems like an eternity," he says, rubbing his thumb across my cheek, "though it's only been a few days."

"An awful few days," I grumble, letting tears well into my eyes. Broin's the only person I would *ever* cry in front of.

He brushes a tear from the corner of my eye. "I know it has been, Little Red." He slides his fingers down to my lips, his touch warm and gentle. "I think we both need this."

My mouth instinctively opens as he rubs a finger along the seam of my lips. He trails his hand to the back of my head and grabs a handful of hair, tilting my head so I'm forced to look up at him.

"You're not a freak," he tells me, his voice dark with conviction, "and you're not contaminated. But you are about to be punished like the bad little witch you are."

"Ooh, Daddy." I grin up at him. "What are you going to do to me?"

In one swift movement, he claims my mouth in a deep, passionate kiss. His stubble tickles my lips as our tongues dance to the lust percolating between us. I step onto my tiptoes, seeking his warmth, his touch as a man. When he pulls away, his eyes are pools of blood that simmer with hunger.

"Take off your shirt. Now."

I nod and do as he says without pausing. That's when I realize the closet has been modified. All the clutter has been moved to one side and there's candles dotted around the room. A familiar piece of furniture sits in the middle of the floor. Broin must have conjured the bench from his cabin. I keep my eyes trained on the leather straps and start to leisurely undo my buttons.

Broin moves away and busies himself with the candles. The muscles in his back writhe as he uses magic to bring more light to the room. I gulp, watching him work and shrug my shirt to the floor. I didn't bother putting on any underwear after my shower. I knew Broin would be removing them, preferably with a knife.

"Drape yourself over the bench," he instructs, his focus still on the candles.

I walk over to the bench, lay flat on the leather surface and throw my arms over side. Not a moment later, Broin's palm is on my ass, lifting my skirt and firmly kneading my skin.

Smack.

The first slap stings so beautifully I let out a gasp.

By the tenth spank, I can barely feel my ass and tears fall from my eyes.

Broin stops to caress my tender skin. "Why are you crying?"

"It just feels so fucking good."

He scoffs. "It's not supposed to feel good." Sliding his hand down my leg, he retrieves my knife from my sock. "It's supposed to hurt. And mind your manners."

I grin, closing my eyes to brace myself for the pain. "Sorry, Daddy."

The tip of the cold blade presses into my thigh. I feel a droplet of blood run down my leg and I moan into the bench. Broin glides the knife up to where his handprint burns on my ass. I wait for him to draw more blood, but after a few moments, I'm yet to feel any pain.

I squirm, deliberately wiggling my ass to entice him.

Another spank, this time so hard that I *really* whimper.

Broin moves around the bench. I tilt my head to peek at him through my lashes.

Without even looking at me, he asks in a dangerously low voice, "What are you being punished for?"

"I broke the academy's rules." The knife presses into my still healing back. I bite down on my lip to suppress my screams. "I... I nearly got expelled." My voice is breaking, my body trembling under him. He leisurely slides the blade up my spine, hitting every tender bump. "I didn't listen to you."

"To who?" he probes, pausing between my shoulder blades.

"Broin Blackstone. My knight."

He pushes the blade underneath a swollen welt. "Go on, Little Red."

"My best friend."

More pressure. More blood. Stars dance over my vision.

"My Daddy," I add with a pleasurable groan.

His hardened cock brushes my hip. "You know your place. I just wish you knew when to do as you're told."

I hold my breath, waiting for him to continue. For a long, painful moment — and not the good kind — he just runs his fingers over my back. He traces the pentagram, the goat's face, the horns and the sigil all over again, his movements painfully slow, deliberately keeping me on edge.

Then he pierces the knife into the edge of the wound and starts to carve.

My screams are instantaneous. I push my mouth into the bench to strangle them. The leather mixes with the salty tears slipping into the corner of my mouth.

With one hand tightening around my neck, his other

hard at work on my back, Broin keeps retracing the sigil. Again and again. It's like he's trying to cut Lucifer's mark out from my flesh, even though we both know that's impossible. Once Lucifer claims one of his children, there's no going back. And right now, I've never been so thankful for him giving me this mark. Broin hacking into it like a cut of meat is the most erotic, pleasurable sensation in the world.

A scream escapes my compressed lips and Broin twists the knife harder. Deeper. My blood oozes down my back, between my legs and around my ankles. It's fucking amazing and I'm delirious. The pain washes away my filthy blood. My darkness, in that moment, is tamed for a while. Sometimes when the pain is severe, it no longer exists. Just like it's doing now. It always comes back, though; that's why they call us the Cursed Ones.

Life is such a beautiful and barbaric thing.

Broin yanks the knife out, and I scream. "What did I say about manners?"

"S...sorry, Daddy. Thank you for punishing me."

Broin shoves his fingers between my legs and pries my lower lips open. "It's what you deserve for disobeying me. For breaking the school rules. For disappointing your Daddy."

Pleased to find that I'm indeed wet, he slaps my pussy hard, then eases a finger inside. He leans down and nibbles the side of my ear, his other hand still on my throat. Choking me. Tormenting me.

Ecstasy builds in the pit of my body. It spreads through my chest and into my toes. Broin rubs my clit with his thumb while kissing my ear, my neck, nipping my skin. I close my eyes, my heart rate accelerating in my ears, and curl my toes.

Just when the spine-tingling pleasure starts to cloud my mind, Broin pulls back, causing my orgasm to vanish instantly.

I let out a frustrated cry. But this is my punishment.

Bad girls don't get to cum.

Broin repeats his torment three times more, each time forcing me to grow more pathetically desperate. I'm panting and flushed and so agitated I can scarcely think when he steps back. I crane my neck to watch him walk around the bench, skimming a finger down my leg as he does so. He lowers himself down and taps my inner thigh.

"Open."

I comply, praying to Satan he'll show mercy.

He doesn't.

And deep down I fucking love that.

In place of his fingers, he uses his tongue to tease my pussy. His stubble scratching my sensitive skin feels utterly amazing. I puncture my teeth into the bench, my moans vibrating through the leather.

"You have a busy night ahead of you," Broin murmurs, his breath tickling my lips. "Are you prepared?"

I writhe on the bench, holding the sides to support my arms. "I need to ask Him for His help, Daddy."

"I know you do." A long, slow lick, from my pussy all the way up to the small of my back. "I'll take you to the hidden door I found today. It will halve your journey to the altar." His tongue circles my clit, flicking the little nub in a way that drives me wild.

Again he stops, the bastard, and again I groan.

He's bringing me to the edge of orgasm only to deny me release. It suddenly makes me regret acting like a bitch today.

"You're always one step ahead," I breathe, subtly

pushing my pussy into his face. "Thank you for looking out for me, Daddy."

He laughs and I imagine him flashing a grin. "When you take our Dark Lord's cock tonight, I want you think of me." He shoves three of his fingers into my pussy, harshly pressing against the sweet spot buried inside. "I want you to remember who your Daddy is. Who controls your body as well as your heart."

That familiar, toe-curling sensation builds again, making me feel as though I'm about to explode over the bench. I clench my thighs, close my eyes, and wait for the release to wash over me. But it doesn't. Of course it doesn't. Broin pulls his fingers out at the last second, straightens to look at me, and wipes my arousal on my face.

"Have you learned your lesson now, Little Red?"

With an exasperated sigh, I let my arms flop down in defeat. "Yes, Daddy Broin."

"Good." He gives my pussy a sharp spank. "Time to get you cleaned up."

A rapid warmth floods through me.

The blood seeps back into my veins, stitching the wound together, but not completely. Broin knows I love to feel my wounds heal gradually. He eases me off the bench and I nearly collapse when my feet touch the floor. The pain, the moments of purity as a result of it, feel incredible. Broin grabs my shirt off the floor and helps me into it. I almost want to giggle when he does up the buttons.

I watch him pop them all into place, wondering why he chose to open Lucifer's mark before punishing me. Was he feeling a little possessive?

Before he pulls away, I take his hand in mine. "You're

the only family I've got left, Broin. I won't ever abandon or lose you. Please know that."

Broin frowns for a moment, his eyes switching between mine. I watch his pulse flicker in his throat as he swallows nervously.

He reaches out and tucks my hair behind my ears. "As Satan is my witness, nothing on this earth will stop me from protecting you. I will always be your knight. I will always belong to you."

I smile at him, my heart swelling with a riot of emotions. "Thank you, Daddy. Now where's this magical door you were talking about?"

Chapter Fourteen

Lockwood

I know my students.

I've been headmaster at Everafter for nearly ten years, and in that time, I've seen all of the misbehavior and heard all of the excuses. Redera Hemlock is a troublemaker, and unless I miss my guess, she's the sort to slip out of her dormitory after curfew. She's already broken two rules today. Breaking a third would give her a trifecta.

I don't appreciate her obvious rebelliousness. I'm willing to put part of it down to the recent murder of her family, because that would certainly make anyone's head spin. But I don't think that's the root cause of her defiance. I think it's something about the girl herself, something much deeper, more personal.

She has darkness in her blood. I don't need to use any magic to see that. She shimmers with power, as well, which is disconcerting in a witch so young. She has secrets upon secrets, this girl.

Well... Don't we all.

I wait in the darkness after curfew and watch the hidden door at the side of the castle. It's a squat, square maintenance access hatch that's hidden behind a dense ornamental shrub. By now, I've learned all of the sneaky entrances and exits. I know this school and all of its buildings, from which floorboards squeak to which bricks conceal hiding places. I've ordered some of the tunnels and escape hatches to be sealed up. But I've left some, too, partially because I think the students benefit from being able to rebel in safe and controlled ways.

Using doors I know to break curfew so they can hook up with other students? Minor infractions in the greater scheme of things, but it gives them confidence to think they're putting one over on me... until I show up at their illicit rendezvous and prove that I'm not as blind as they think I am. I'll give them rope, but not enough to hang themselves.

Hanging is obviously a tender subject where Miss Hemlock is concerned. I know what happened to her family and I know who did it. Witch hunting is not an isolated profession in this part of the world. Ever since the Silva War, the Queen of Fantasia - the largest kingdom in the bright half of the Great Forest, where Everafter is located - has encouraged her men-at-arms to hunt down and destroy Darkbloods. She even created a so-called knighthood, the Falcon Knights, who are little more than armored thugs who ride the countryside hunting witches. Their methods are violent and horrifying, but even they can't rival the group that killed Redera's family.

The hunters who destroyed the Hemlocks were in fact wolves. The Rosso Lupa Pack are the stuff of nightmares to people all across Draoich and the Western Forest. They're even harder to bear once you get to know them. The attack on the Hemlock cottage had all of the hallmarks of a Rosso Lupa raid.

I should know. I've seen them operate up close.

The door that I've been watching slowly opens. I make myself one with the shadows and watch carefully. Hemlock emerges, clad in a scarlet-red cloak. She looks around but doesn't see me. She's satisfied that she's alone and trots off through the gate and out toward the forest.

Why is a young girl going into the forest alone in the dead of night?

No good will come of it, I'm certain. There are hundreds of things that she might encounter in the darkness, even on this "blessed" side of the Great Forest. She could very well be walking into a danger that she can't walk out of.

Knowing the chances of this are high, I follow her. I use my wand to activate the Soundless Passing spell on my boots, allowing me to walk through the underbrush almost silently. Hemlock doesn't hear me. She keeps walking and I keep following.

Her path is long and arduous. She goes deep into the wood, almost to the edge of the Black Ravine, and I realize where she's headed. The girl turns before she reaches that scar in the earth's face and heads north. I follow her until she reaches a clearing ringed with standing stones. In the center of the clearing is a stone altar with grooves carved around its edges to catch and direct sacrificial blood. The darkest of dark magic is practiced in this place. They call it the Devil's Altar.

I know better than to step inside the circle. I can feel the dark magic that emanates from the cold granite and it makes me shiver. I sense a powerful evil approaching and I would be lying if I said I wasn't concerned. Hemlock seems unbothered, though, and her face is almost serene as she turns to face a black cloud that flutters into the circle to join her. I crouch behind the underbrush, watching but trying not to be seen.

The cloud swirls around the altar, then solidifies into a single column of darkness right in front of the girl. The stench of sulfur is intense and it stings my nose. It's all I can do not to cough. She lifts her chin and watches as the column transforms into a man in a golden robe. But this is no ordinary man. He radiates stunning amounts of power and evil and my heart is beating so hard I wonder if they can hear it in the clearing.

The man turns and walks slowly around the altar while she speaks to him. Underneath his open robe, he's naked. He also has the legs of a goat with cloven hooves that leave scorched prints everywhere he steps.

I know who this powerful entity is, and the thought that I'm actually looking upon the Fallen One is nearly incomprehensible.

He stops circling and takes her face in his hand. Their mouths move though I can't hear a single word. There's an obvious tension between them, but not the kind that comes from arguing. Theirs is the kind that comes from trying not to ravage one another senseless. The sexual spark between the two is palpable and I'm already hard. My dick is throbbing. I try to ignore it, but that's a fight I'm destined to lose.

Hemlock smiles, and it's the filthiest smile I've ever seen. Or maybe it just inspires me to want to do dirty things. It seems to have affected Satan the same way, because he seizes her in his arms and kisses her, hard. He turns her around and bends her over the altar, and... I move around the clearing to get a better view.

What the fuck is wrong with me?

I've never been a voyeur before, but when he bends

Hemlock over the altar and pulls her skirt up to her waist, I can't tear my eyes away. He dumps his robe on the ground. His rampant erection is enormous and he wastes no time with subtlety or foreplay before he buries it in her quivering flesh. I wince, thinking how much that penetration has to hurt, and Hemlock gasps, but then she lets out a moan that makes my own cock twitch.

I find myself wishing it was me buried up to the hilt in her tight cunt.

As soon as I have that thought, I try to force it away.

She's one of my students! What am I thinking?

He starts fucking her like with ruthless abandon, and she *loves* it. His hands sprout long claws and batlike wings extend out from his back, growing as I watch. I'm simultaneously horrified, fascinated and turned on more than I've ever been in my thirty-two years.

I give in to impulse and unbutton my pants. My own erection springs forth and I take it in my hand. At that moment, Satan's glowing golden eyes turn in my direction and he grins. He changes his angle so I can see his cock sinking into her dripping pussy. I should be horrified—disgusted—but I'm not. I watch his thrusts and the way the ferocity of his fucking rocks her whole body.

This is agony.

He grins and alters his angle again, grabbing her by the waist and pulling her feet off the ground so he can rail her pussy. He's pushing the air out of her in gasps and my hand is rubbing my cock in time with the pistoning that he's laying down. She screams, her passion tumbling from her throat. He slams into her once, twice, and then he's cumming, too. I can see his heavy balls contracting as he pumps her full of his seed.

The sounds, the smells, the sight... It's all too much.

I shoot my load over the bushes, my legs contracting and breaths coming out rapid. I want to be him. I want to be buried in that hot little body, filling her cunt with my spunk. I want to be the one to make her scream like that, the one leaving handprint bruises on her hip bones.

I want to own this girl.

A voice speaks in my head. *So own her.*

Satan pulls free and puts her back on her feet. He smacks her on the ass and gathers up his robe. I try to hide, but it's useless. I know he knows I'm here. I just need to make sure that Hemlock doesn't see me. Satan vanishes into smoke and I'm left crouched here like an oversexed teenager, my dripping cock still hard in my hand, my heart pounding with need.

The need for *her*.

It takes me a long moment to gather myself. I withdraw my handkerchief from my pocket and wipe my fingers and cock with it, cleaning away my jizz before I tuck myself back into my trousers. I need to concentrate. I need to remember who I am and why I came here. I'm the headmaster of Everafter Academy. Hemlock is my student. My goal had not been to spy on her having sex with the Devil - the Devil! - and whack off to it. It was to learn what Redera Hemlock is up to, and I certainly have my answer now.

She's a Satanist.

And I just shot my load to her getting fucked by her dark god.

The fuck is wrong with me?

I've seen and done a lot of shit in my life, but this has to be the worst.

She takes longer to compose herself than I do. I don't

blame her. I'd be insensible if I was a woman who'd been fucked that hard by a dick that big.

Confession: I'm a little jealous of the Dark One's tool.

Shit. I'm going fucking insane.

I take a deep breath and gather my thoughts. What I've seen here is confirmation that Redera Hemlock is no white witch. Quite the contrary. She's as dark as they come - no pun intended.

I retreat from the forest and teleport back to the school. The darkness inside me that I thought I had expunged is singing and it takes all my might to shove it aside. I cannot go back to being what I was, and yet, watching her tonight, I wonder what more I could still be.

It's nothing but ruinous folly to think this way. Excuses aside, I should be ashamed of myself for what I've done tonight. I *am* horrified with myself. I'm also shocked that someone of her ilk has found her way into my school.

How did I miss that?

I stand in the shadows near the secret door she'll undoubtedly use to sneak back into the school. After a long while, I see her coming back, walking swiftly along the path with a spring in her step. Frankly, I'm surprised she can even walk after the pounding she just took.

She's almost to the bushes when I step out in front of her, startling her half to death. She doesn't scream and she doesn't react with shame. Her first instinct is to drop into what's basically a fighter's crouch, then her eyes widen.

"It seems I now know who and what you really are, Miss Hemlock. Come with me."

I seize her by the upper arm and she lets me. Magic tingles everywhere I touch her and I want to shake her until that excess power goes away. I want to shake myself awake.

Chapter Fifteen

Ravyn

I follow Lockwood, cursing my luck the whole way. He saw me with Lucifer and now he knows beyond a shadow of a doubt what I am. He knows I'm a dark witch and he knows I don't belong in his school. He's going to expel me. I'll never find out who the wolf at Everafter is and I'll never find out about Esmeralda. Worst of all, I'll have disappointed my Dark Lord, and he's not someone you want to disappoint.

This is a fucking disaster.

I just wanted to ask Lucifer for the ability to scry so I could look for the Russo Lupa Pack. I also wanted to be able to communicate with Esmeralda. He said he'd give me both and we sealed the deal. When he was done, he told me that Lockwood had been watching the entire time.

Fucking pervert.

Strangely, Lucifer wasn't overly concerned, even though this could be the end of my career at Everafter. In fact, it gave my lord an idea to hatch a plan, and as you'd expect, it's diabolical. Hopefully I won't have to use it. Hopefully Lockwood will show me mercy, though, going by his grip on my arm, I highly doubt it.

We get to a spot in the forest that's full of white magic. It makes my skin itch. Up overhead, the moon shines brightly, just shy of being full. Its light lets me see the fierce look on Lockwood's face as he stops and turns to me.

"I knew that you would break curfew," he says, his tone caustic. "Your kind always do."

"My kind?" I echo, annoyed at the jab.

"Trouble makers."

"And you always follow trouble makers around?" I ask, putting on a front. I'm scared and upset, which always makes me snappish. How could I have been so stupid?

Lockwood takes a step closer and I take one back. "I make it my job to know everything that goes on at my school, including any potential threats," he replies, his eyes boring into me.

"You see me as a threat?" I keep walking until my back thuds into a tree.

"I see you as a rule breaker. A disruption. A bad influence."

His words send a crippling wave of anxiety through me. I grasp at the tree, digging my fingers into the bark. My stomach twists into a knot and I look away, wondering how in the name of Satan I can get my headmaster to keep me on at his precious school. But then I notice something rather interesting.

Something that stacks the odds in my favor.

"Is being a bad influence really so bad, Sir?" I glance down at his erection, which he sheepishly and very swiftly hides with his cloak. "Looks like you're enjoying it."

A slight tinge rises to his cheeks.

I glide up to him, my eyes locked on him like a predator on its prey. The dynamic between us has transformed and I'm not going to let it change back. My true colors rise to the surface, letting my dark witch free. She yawns and stretches her arms inside me, pleased to be out of her cage for a while. With a cruel smile, she takes control of the situation and I let her.

"I know you were watching," I tell him, pulling my lips into a smug grin. His pupils are blown and I'm close enough that if I angle my hip just right, I can brush against his wood. He sucks in air through his nose. "Did watching Satan fuck my tight hole turn you on, Sir?"

He steps back, his face darkening in the moonlight. "You do not belong at Everafter. After what I've seen, I should expel you immediately."

Should is the keyword there.

"But you're not going to, are you, Sir?" I close the gap between us and reach down for his cock. He pulls away before I can touch him. Tease.

"Why are you here?" His tone is clipped, hoping to convey a false sense of calmness. But I can hear every erratic beat of his heart, every nervous intake of breath. He's both anxious and aroused, conflicted and desperate. I go in for the kill.

"I'm here to get an education, of course. And to learn how to be a good girl." I step forward again, brushing my fingers over his cock. "Don't you want me to be a good girl, Sir?"

He doesn't back up. In fact, he doesn't move at all. "Your kind belongs at Nevermore."

Again with that superficial voice. I smirk at him. "What? Where fairytales never come true, Sir? How fortunate for me."

I turn my hand so my palm is against his dick. It's hard and I can imagine the precum pooling on the head. My mouth waters at the thought. I wish I could see him. I satisfy myself with taking a feel instead.

"Miss Hemlock..." He sucks his teeth, his breath catching in his throat. "That's enough."

I stroke him again and he groans. I lean in close, tipping my head up because he's so much taller. "Do you know what I think, Professor Lockwood? I think you want to fuck me. I think you saw Satan tearing up my pussy and you wished it was you. I think that if I gave you the chance, that's exactly what you'd do." I rub harder, giving his cock a light squeeze. "Right. Now."

I lean up to kiss him and to my surprise, he doesn't pull away. In fact, he kisses me back, his tongue spearing into my mouth in a pale imitation of what he'd really like to do to me. I grab his tongue between my teeth and bite it gently, then suck on it for a moment. He groans into my mouth.

When I let go and step back, I can't help but chuckle. "Looks like I have some dirt on you, now, don't I? What would your Storyteller - or the High Council - say about you kissing one of your students, I wonder?"

His rapid heartbeat freezes. "Who are you, really?"

I shrug indifferently. "Just Ravyn Hemlock of the She'ol Clan."

"Vampires?"

"Dark witches," I correct him, "but cursed all the same. Don't worry, Sir. I'm not here to drink your blood. I want your silence."

Lockwood's face turns scarlet with rage again, matching the shade of my own cloak. "Are you blackmailing me, girl?"

A derisive grin blossoms over my face. "Well, I *am* a villain, aren't I? I'm not like the other girls in this school."

He grinds his teeth. "Clearly."

"I think you like that about me." I press against him and he still doesn't pull away. His muscles are taut as a bowstring. I push onto my tiptoes and brush my fingers against his neatly-trimmed beard. "I think you're tired of princesses and do-gooders and the happy-ever-after crowd. You've got darkness inside you. I can smell it. And I think you've been wanting a bad girl to keep you company."

He swallows hard, the pulse in his throat fluttering like a caged bird. "You think this game will work?"

"I don't think, I know. I'm the bad girl you've been waiting for." I brush my lips against the corner of his jaw. "When I'm good, I'm bad. But when I'm bad? I'll blow your fucking mind, Sir. Why don't you let me show you?"

For all his pointless bravado, I know Lockwood is still a man at the end of the day and men always react the same. I should know; I've spent eighteen years controlled by His Excellency. Lockwood will never get his emotions settled down as long as I'm holding his cock. It's not like he's trying to take it back, anyway.

A grin plays on my lips. I've got him right where I need him, just like Lucifer told me I would. But then Lockwood's hand is around my throat, the other seizing my wrist, and my smirk vanishes.

He leans in, bringing his lips to my ear. "I don't take kindly to blackmailers. If you knew what was good for you, witch, you wouldn't push me. I guarantee you'll live to regret it."

I chuckle in the back of my throat, the movement slightly constricted by his hand. "You like being called 'Sir,' don't you? I'll bet that deep inside, you're a Master just looking for the perfect little Slave."

His grip tightens. I also put pressure on his cock and

dig my fingernails in, but he doesn't even flinch. Fuck, that's hot.

"I think you want to punish me for being a bad girl," I tell him. "Breaking curfew and polluting your precious school with my dark self. It disgusts you." Rubbing his cock harder, I watch him intently, waiting for a change in his expression. He doesn't falter, but his cock answers me well, standing to full attention under his silk pants. "Wouldn't you like to bend me over your knee and spank me until my ass is bright red? Don't you want to shove your hard cock down my throat and skull fuck me until I can no longer breathe? Maybe you'd like to do what headmasters always do best and cane the sin out of me."

Lockwood shoves me back, still clenching my throat, and pushes me up against the tree. My feet dangle off the ground. All the while, his lips move against mine in a violent, passionate, all-consuming rage. His free hand slides over my breasts, down my front, between my legs, grabbing my pussy. I moan and gasp into his mouth, seizing his hair for support.

But then he disappears and I fall down with a thud, landing on my already sore ass. He's nowhere to be seen, and the woods are quiet once again. That motherfucker must have translocated back into the school. I guess he wanted to think about my offer in private.

No matter. I know he's going to say yes.

Men like him can never resist temptation. It's in their blood.

Chapter Sixteen

Ravyn

As soon as Lockwood is gone, Broin drops down from the tree and lands beside me as a man. He's still only wearing his pants, though he's pulled on some boots and fuck if he doesn't look delectable.

"That was an interesting conversation," he comments, a bitter edge to his voice.

I straighten off the ground, brushing the leaves from my clothes. "I'm merely doing what I need to do to survive this stupid place."

"So you're using him?"

I think for a moment, trying hard not to let my other side fill me with guilt. With my dark blood polluting her veins, I wonder if Redera ever felt like this, torn between good and bad? Or did choosing come naturally to her?

"I'm just having a little fun," I answer honestly, because it isn't a lie.

"Haven't you had enough fun?"

"There's never enough fun," I grin, the two of us fully aware that Lucifer's cum is inside me, a delightful, burning sensation. "Just enough for tonight."

He shakes his head. "You're a naughty girl, Little Red."

"Oh, bite me, Daddy," I laugh, winking at him.

Broin takes my hand and we stroll through the dark wood together.

He watched me with Lucifer, then he watched me with Professor Lockwood. He seems to be taking things better than I imagined. But I know just from his quietness that he's troubled. How is he really taking all this? In a matter of a few days, our lives have changed in ways neither of us imagined or even wanted. For the past year, I've belonged solely to Broin, and while he never minded multiple partners before, things have irrevocably changed.

It's not uncommon for our coven to have multiple mates; the Dark Lord encourages it. Satanalia, the time of sexual indulgence and physical worship among our clan, happens regularly at the Church of Shadows. They're celebrated like Fantasia celebrates the Festival of Light, only ours occur at the beginning of each season when the moon is ripe. I'm sure the first moon of autumn is next week, which means I'll have no choice but to face His Excellency. If he did find out — and I imagine Lucifer would have told him — that I tried to leave his coven, his wrath will be unlike anything I've ever seen.

The kind I'm *not* looking to.

Hopefully, under the circumstances, he'll allow me to sit this one out. I've spent every Satanalia with him since I was sixteen. His emotional and physical scars are still etched into my bones. He's the cruellest and most powerful of the clan. My body shudders and recoils at the memories. I crave and fear them.

I squeeze Broin's hand. "Satanalia is coming up soon, isn't it?"

He glances at me from the corner of his eyes. "Yes. Do you wish to go?"

"Heaven no. The thought of facing everyone, after what I did..."

"You'll have to face them sooner or later," he points out. "You're still a member of this clan. None of the covens will forgive you if you try to avoid them."

I open my mouth to dispute the matter, then snap my jaw shut. My family has been dead for two days, and not once has any member of the clan tried to contact me. Our coven never even sent a raven to pass on their condolences. Broin knows this and falls quiet. The normally comfortable silence is heavy, laden with tension that stretches between us. He hasn't been right since we came here.

I come to a halt, letting go of his hand, "What's wrong?"

Broin looks away, unable to hold my gaze. His cheeks are flushing in the moonlight. "You know how I feel about sharing you like this."

"You've shared me before, with His Excellency."

"Not like this."

His pained voice is killing me. I reach out to turn his face around, but he takes hold of my wrist.

"It's sharing you with people I don't know that kills me, Little Red. People I don't trust."

"What are you afraid of?" I breathe, my heart warm from his affection.

"When you're with them, I'm not there to protect you. What if something happens? What if I'm not there to save you? If I lose you..." His voice cracks and he clenches his jaw, unable to finish his sentence.

I know he isn't referring to Lucifer or His Excellency.

He's talking about Lockwood.

I touch his face with my fingertips, his hand still

locked on my wrist. "Nothing will ever take you away from me. Even after the four years are up, even after I avenge my family, nothing will separate us."

"What if—"

"You told me to never focus on the what ifs," I cut in, using my other hand to untangle his grip so I can slide my fingers through his. "You said it just veils us from the present. That it's an illusion meant to trap us."

"It does." His expression softens. "It is."

"Then please don't torment yourself. I know what I'm doing. The Dark Lord has a plan that will help the both of us. Trust me. Trust us."

Standing on my toes to kiss him on the lips, I wrap my arms around his neck and hold him close. His arm slips around my waist and he embraces me. I always feel safe in his hands—hands that are capable of such destruction and yet love at the same time.

When we emerge from the woods some moments later, he shifts into his raven and flies up to my shoulder. I look around before approaching the hidden door. I've already been exposed once tonight. My body is aching, my insides throbbing from Lucifer's ravishment. I don't think I have any energy to fight off another spectator.

In my exhaustion, as I step out of the closet and walk down the hallway, I realize I never cast a glamour. But it's too late. Christopher, walking toward me in his pajamas, jerks to a halt. The grey owl on his shoulder gawps at me.

I turn away in an attempt to avoid him.

"Hey, wait a minute."

Letting out a heavy sigh, I swing around with my hands on my hips. "What's up?" His pajamas are covered in llamas that make me smirk. "Nice getup."

A grin lights up his handsome face. "I saw you sticking up for Quasimodo."

"And?" I can't help but sound defensive. It's not that I hate Christopher, I just don't trust him. "Have you come to tell me I should be hanged for helping other people? If so, save your breath."

He shakes his head, his long hair swaying from side to side. "Nah. I actually want to thank you."

"Thank... me?" I repeat the words, raising a sceptical brow.

"Yeah. What you did for him was noble of you."

I nearly laugh at the statement. There's nothing noble about me. But I can't deny that I'm surprised by him. Actually, when I think about it, he's never wronged me. It's only Gideon and Erik who have it out for me, along with their three bimbos.

"Sorry if any of the soup splashed you yesterday," I say sheepishly. "I was only aiming for Gideon."

He laughs. "Trust me. I've used worse hair masks."

"Oh yeah? Like what."

"You don't want to know," he warns, wiggling his nose in disgust.

"Well, like I said, I was aiming for Gideon anyway."

"Yeah, about that..." Now it's Christopher's turn to look sheepish. He runs a hand through his glossy hair. It's unfair for a dude to have such beautiful locks. "Gideon isn't what he makes himself out to be."

I roll my eyes. "Let me guess. He puts on a front because he's secretly insecure?"

He lifts his eyebrows. "That's exactly it."

Sure it is.

"Why did you take the blame for him?"

Christopher pauses, thinking for a second. "Because without him I wouldn't be here."

I don't get a chance to ask why. The devil in question appears in the hallway. Unlike Christopher, he isn't wearing any cute pajamas. His ripped torso is on full display with just a pair of sweatpants hugging his waist. He's leaner than I expected, and in the dimly lit hallway, his pale skin looks bronze. I peel my eyes off the sex lines sliding under his pants. There's something super fucking hot about that little V.

I grimace at my own thoughts, reminding myself who this is. Gideon, Prince of Assholes.

"Snake girl," he greets spitefully. "What are you doing out at this time? Sacrificing a goat?"

"No. I'm looking for a virgin to sacrifice, actually. Don't suppose you'd like to offer yourself?"

A tinge of blood seeps into his face, reddenning his features. This guy is simply too easy to wind up.

"Let's go," he tells Christopher, barging by me. "Let the Darkblood get in trouble for all I care."

I watch the boys walk down the hallway. Christopher glances over his shoulder to give an amused grin, which I surprisingly return in good humor. When he looks away, I glare into the back of Gideon's head. The best thing about all this is that he doesn't expect girls to stand up to him. He's used to people following him around like a flock of sheep. But he's forgetting one very important thing. I'm the wolf in sheep's clothing and I'm not afraid to put him in his place. I just need to be more subtle about it until I hear Lockwood's answer.

Hopefully, everything goes according to the Dark Lord's plan...

Chapter Seventeen

Ravyn

I wake up feeling less exhausted than I did yesterday. I guess getting fucked senseless helped with that. Nothing quite beats a good workout.

Stretching my arms out, I carefully sit up in bed, mindful of my back, and every other part of my body that are all kinds of sore. I look around with a lazy yawn, hoping Alice has come back from the infirmary.

"Oh my fuck!" I shriek out, coming face to face with her.

She's sitting on the edge of my bed, watching me with her big, wide eyes. "Did you sleep well?"

I clutch my blankets in mock distress. "Alice. Were you watching me sleep?"

"I made breakfast," she says. "Sirena told me what happened. That Rapunzel is such a *nasty bitch*. Now you don't have to go to the cafeteria!"

Pointing to the tray at the foot of my bed, which Broin is cautiously inspecting, I find two slices of massacred bread, an entire raw carrot (still covered in dirt), a glass of questionable milk, and what I think is supposed to be bacon. She's an awful cook, just like Redera.

"Wow. You made me all that?" I smile with genuine fondness and reach over to grab a slice of bread. It's burnt to a crisp, but I don't let that stop me from eating. The last thing I want to do is hurt my friend's feelings. Satan knows I've eaten worse. "I don't mind going, though. Challenging Prince Biff and his wannabe gang keeps me on my toes. It's exciting."

Alice giggles. The bags under her eyes are heavier and darker than when I met her. "Well, I just figured we could eat breakfast here."

"Plus," Sirena says, stepping out of the ensuite with her hair wrapped in a towel, "this morning's a study class. We get to hang out and create havoc." She winks at me before returning to the bathroom.

Alice shouts back at her, "Study days do actually mean that we study."

"Spoil sport," Sirena grumbles and Alice rolls her eyes.

I take a bite of the toast and nearly crack a tooth. "So," I start, swallowing down the mouthful of razors, "where should we study?"

Alice thinks for a moment. "Oh! We could go to the library. We're even allowed to bring our familiars there, so long as they behave."

"Then let's go!" I throw my legs over the bed and stand up. Realizing I'm still in Sirena's tank top and pajama pants, I laugh. "Err, once I'm dressed that is."

"And don't forget to finish your breakfast," Alice reminds me as I walk over to the bathroom.

"What are you trying to do? Kill her?" Sirena asks, opening the door. "You don't really have to eat it, you know. Her heart is in the right place but her cooking is terrible."

Alice throws a pillow at Sirena's face. "Hey, I heard

that!"

"What? It's true."

My body fills with warmth at their exchange. Compared to last night's events, this is a breath of fresh air. It's the sort of light I don't mind basking in to balance out the darkness for a while.

ONCE I SHOWER AND PUT ON A FRESH UNIFORM, THE three of us head to the library. Sirena is carrying the basket she brought me, and I think it's filled with snacks for lunch. Hopefully Alice hasn't cooked any of it, though I appreciate the gesture. I'm able to grow a lot of things back with magic but teeth aren't one of them.

Jasper hops through the courtyard ahead of us. It's a scorching day and students are sprawled out on the grass, some reading books, others soaking up the sun. Familiars prance around them and I can't help but smile. I'm thankful we're allowed to bring our familiars to the library. At least there they don't have to be on their own.

The library is located in one of the round towers. As opposed to Lockwood's office in the West Tower, we're headed to the east part of the castle. The stairs are predictably long and steep, the windows the same circular shape as the other towers'. But the interior is unexpectedly darker. Floor-to-ceiling tapestries hang between the windows, the gilded frames capturing the light. One of the landscape paintings even moves when we walk by and I'm convinced the waterfall is a portal.

There must be tons of hidden portals in this castle. Maybe I should start looking for them. I'm not really a fan of spending alone time with Broin in a closet for four whole years. Maybe a portal would give us someplace more stimulating to go.

But then I remember that students aren't allowed to access portals. I want to pout.

As we climb the seemingly endless stairs, I look at the sun gleaming across Lake Annan. It's beautiful, with not a cloud in the sky above, and the far distance is made up of rolling green hills. When Broin and I hunted back home, we used to climb the highest tree we could find and watch the moonrise over that same lake.

A sharp pang wrenches my heart. I reach up and stroke Broin's feathers.

—*What's wrong?*— *he asks in a worried tone.*

—*Nothing. Just feeling nostalgic.*—

—*The lake?*—

I nod. —*Yeah, the lake.*—

Alice points to a butterfly archway at the top of the stairs. She's smiling and hurrying toward it. It's good to see her fit and happy again.

Broin says, —*One day we'll be back up in that tree, Little Red.*—

I hope he's right.

We walk through the arch into the library. My jaw drops at the towering bookshelves covering every inch of the walls. The ceiling is domed, like all the round towers here, and the sun pouring through the glass shoots rays of light across the room.

This is by far my favorite room in the castle.

Some other students are already sitting at benches, poring over old books and parchments. In the far corner, where the sofas and armchairs are nestled around a rustic fireplace, a desk of computers sit unoccupied. That always surprises me. It's like having a car in the middle of the stone age. I highly doubt I'd even be able to turn the thing on.

Sirena skips over to the bench pushed up against a large spherical window. The lake is visible from this angle and the view is utterly breath-taking. Figures that Sirena likes to be close to water whenever she can. Alice and I follow her to the bench. Above the window, a huge map of our world hovers in the air. Each kingdom shimmers like burnished jewels, emblazoned with all the names of the royals and the members of the High Council.

I set my bag on the table and read the list of royal names. Until now, I've never cared about the other kingdoms because She'ol was all I've been taught to concern myself with. We have a coven based in each of the kingdoms, but it's only their Churches of Shadows that I've visited. I'm genuinely curious to find out which princes and princesses belong where.

Erik is Prince of Aira in the north east. It's a maritime kingdom on the beautiful harbor that overlooks the Capsian Sea. I've only been there once, but I was pleasantly surprised. Next is Aurora, Princess of Talia, which I already knew. Cinder is Princess of Wysteria, one of the smallest kingdoms nestled in the Western Mountains. Apparently it's being governed by her step-mother until Cinder comes of age. I'm surprised to find Rapunzel listed with Christopher as Princess and Prince of Fantasia. I never knew they were siblings. They look and act nothing alike.

I search the list for Gideon but he doesn't seem to be there. He is a prince, isn't he? That's weird... Oh, and Draoich is missing from the map.

Obviously.

A beautiful young woman with tawny brown hair

sweeps by the window. She's holding a stack of books to her chest and smiles at every student she passes.

Sirena catches me looking and explains, "That's the librarian, Mrs. Beauty. I heard her husband was mauled by wolves."

Alice grimaces. "That's not what I was told by Nurse Darling. She said Mrs. Beauty's husband was a wolf and he fought in the war."

This catches my interest. I try to feign innocence as I don't want them to find out why I'm really here. "Aren't wolves forbidden? I thought they were only allowed in Draoich."

"Yup." Sirena sets the basket on the table and flops into a chair. "The last wolf hasn't been sighted over the border for…"

"Ten years," Alice finishes off, sitting beside her. "You have a terrible memory."

"Well excuse me. I was only, what, eight at the time? I don't have a photographic memory like you do. You're lucky that way."

Alice frowns at the table, whispering, "I wouldn't call it lucky."

I don't know what Alice has gone through. But the fact that she came from Underland and survived to tell the tale already speaks volumes about her past.

Underland is the land of nightmares.

A strange urge to hug her consumes me again. I brush it off, not wanting to appear weirder than I already have, and sit across from them. I take out my books and Broin hops on one of them while Jasper scurries underneath the table.

It's strangely comfortable working beside my new friends. I've never had many before I came here. Actually,

I think the most I've had is four, and three of them were Redera, Grandma and Broin. Five more if you count Redera's chickens.

They were probably cooked to a crisp in the fire, poor little bastards. I regret not checking on them. They were Redera's pets, after all. I'd just assumed everything had been destroyed before the fire was even lit. The wolves are generous like that. Find everything, leave nothing.

"I've already told you. I'm not interested," a girl says behind me, her voice gentle and softly spoken. "You're far too young for me."

"You say that, but I bet if you took a ride on my magic carpet, you'd think otherwise."

Amused, I turn halfway to watch their exchange. I'm already rooting for the girl. There's nothing more hilarious than watching a dude who can't take a hint get shot down.

The girl turns out to be Mrs. Beauty.

Picking up another book abandoned on another bench, she shakes her head at the boy. "Nothing you could ever say will convince me of that, Aladdin. Please go back to your studies."

The boy huffs, blowing his dark unruly hair away from his eyes and steps in front of her. "Come on. One ride and I promise to shut up? I have good chat. Really I do. You wouldn't believe half the things I've done."

"And we have a bragger," I mutter, rolling my eyes.

Alice and Sirena, overhearing me, look up from their work to eavesdrop too.

"You're *far* too young for me," Mrs. Beauty repeats "I'm sorry."

She tries to step around him, but he blocks her path, causing my hackles to rise. If he doesn't take the hint, I swear to Satan I will bitch slap the life out of him.

"Don't you want to hear some of the secrets I know? You wouldn't believe the gossip I have on the students here. And I've even been to Nevermore. Yup. I went there on my carpet."

If this guy's head gets any bigger he'll take off like a balloon.

"Quit lying," Mrs. Beauty says softly. "And please let me get back to work."

When she tries to walk away again and he grabs her arm, I throw my legs off the bench and prepare to get up. Satan knows why I'm feeling protective of someone I don't even know. I wish this Aladdin would just take the hint and quit while he's ahead.

"I do know something you should probably know."

Mrs. Beauty looks more intrigued than irritated now. "What's that?"

"Yesterday, when I was here — you remember, I brought the flowers?"

"Those were weeds," she counters dryly. "But thank you for the effort."

His face lights up like a puppy who's just been called a good boy. "It was my pleasure, Mrs. Beauty. Anything for a beautiful damsel."

She shakes her head at him. "You were saying about yesterday?"

"Oh. Yeah. Well, I was hanging out back there." He points a thumb over his shoulder, indicating the rows of books. "And heard these two kids talking. Hansel and Metal or something."

"Gretl," Mrs. Beauty corrects him, laughing. "What did they say?"

"The girl, Metal, Gretl, whatever, started crying. I asked them what was wrong and do you know what they said? Do you?" He pauses for effect.

"Hurry up and spit it out, dammit," Sirena mutters, loud enough for Aladdin to glance over at us and frown.

The girls go back to their books, pretending they totally weren't eavesdropping. I just wink at him which he returns with an amused grin.

Mrs. Beauty finally manages to escape him and walks away.

"Hey, wait. I wasn't finished!" Aladdin scurries after her, bypassing a group of students throwing nuts into a monkey's mouth. The creature is sitting on the bench as though he's the Lord of the Land and these students are his servants. The students think it's hilarious.

Once Aladdin has caught up to her, I use my advanced hearing to focus on their conversation.

"What do you want, Aladdin?"

"Just a date. One night, me and you."

Beauty pauses as if she's really considering the possibility. "You know I can't. I work here and dating students is against the rules."

"But what if told you that there's a wolf hiding in this school? A student. Would that change your mind? We could go hunting for them."

"A-a wolf?" she echoes incredulously. "What do you mean?"

"Told you. Secrets. I have a whole cave of them."

Aladdin couldn't sound more smug if he tried.

But is what he said true? Is that why Gretl was crying, because she saw a wolf at Everafter Academy? I'm not sure Aladdin is a reliable source, but he's all I've got.

I look down at Broin. —*Did you hear all that?*—

—*It looks like we've got our lead, Little Red.*—

Chapter Eighteen

Ravyn

Despite all the excitement, I do manage to get some studying done before lunch. Sirena opens the basket, takes out a bunch of boxes and sets them on the table. We share the sandwiches and Sirena hands me a bottle of orange juice. I'm delighted to see she's also included some candy. As I devour the chocolatey goodness, I make a mental note to conjure some dinner later. It's the least I can do to pay back their kindness.

After lunch, we take our familiars back to our room. I'm almost too excited to wait until the day's over when I can find Aladdin and finally get some answers. I try not to get my hopes up but it's hard when so much is at stake. If what Aladdin said is true and he knows who the student is, this could save me months of tracking down Rosso Lupa with little to no progress. I just hope he isn't full of bullshit.

I walk to potions with Sirena, my eyes on the floor as we weave through the castle. Sirena is talking about her home, and how the capital, Delphina, was named after her late mother. I try my best to listen to her but my thoughts keep straying. I feel sick with excitement, though it's not only about Aladdin. I'm eager to hear what Professor Lockwood has to say about last night. So far I haven't seen him or his eagle hanging around. Let's hope he doesn't leave me hanging for too long. I need pain, the kind I know he can deliver.

We enter the class and grab the nearest empty seats. Even though I like Professor Rumpkin, the class itself is so fucking basic that I want to pull my hair out by the roots. Speaking of hair, I'm just getting settled when Rapunzel comes flouncing in with the rest of the princess posse. Gideon and Erik, as usual, trail along behind.

"Hey, Medusa," I greet, and Sirena giggles. "I didn't think you were in this class."

She's trying to stifle a smile, but it just makes her look like more of a simpering idiot. I can see that she has something in her hand hidden between her overly-ample chest and the books she's holding.

"I am now," she said.

Aurora stands back, giving Rapunzel room. This doesn't bode well.

With a look of triumph, impressed with her own cleverness, Rapunzel pulls out a wand made of willow wood and points it at me. It's skinny and has no core, which means it's mostly useless. I hope whoever sold her this piece of crap is having a good laugh.

"*Pustulis correptus!*" she blurts.

A flash of yellow-green light arcs out of the end of the wand. It's not even moving very fast. I hold up my hand and block the tiny lightning with my palm, my face deadpan, and the spell to cause acne falls away like grey dust.

Inside, however, I'm furious.

Nobody hexes a Hemlock!

"You're lucky I didn't turn that back on you," I snarl, rising slowly off my seat.

"I think you should," Sirena coaxes. "She deserves it."

I want to laugh, but I'm so angry that every hair on my head shivers and I'm seeing red. Rapunzel falls back toward Gideon, who manfully steps away from her so she can't hide behind him. All of her so-called friends back away from her, trying to get out of the blast zone of my retaliation.

There won't be any. Lockwood's eagle flies into the room and lands on the back of the chair beside me, its red eyes flicking over the assembled students. He's sizing up the situation and will no doubt report back to his master. If I cast anything now, I'll end up expelled for sure. I grind my teeth and force myself to stand down.

The eagle looks at me and speaks in my mind. —*You will see Professor Lockwood immediately.*—

—*What about my classes?*— I ask.

The eagle makes a sound like laughter. —*We all know you don't need this class, Ravyn.*—

I don't expect him to call me by my real name, but I suppose if Lockwood knows my secrets, then his familiar does, too.

—*Tell him I'm on my way. Please.*—

The bird spreads its wings. —*Don't make him wait.*—

I gather up my books and shove them into my bag. "Guess you just lucked out, Medusa."

"You're the lucky one," Gideon tells me. "If you'd hexed her again, we'd be within our rights to string you up as the Darkblood you are."

I want to stab him in the eye. Instead I turn to Sirena, who's lifting a fist at Gideon, her hair growing red from her roots down. I grab her arm to stop her, not wanting my friend to get in trouble because of me.

"I've gotta go. See you later?"

She rests her arm and nods, keeping her eyes pinned on Gideon. I wave at the bullies and leave the classroom, hoping just a little bit that she does smack him. His smug face deserves it more than anyone.

My heart is pounding with excitement as I make my way to Lockwood's tower. I'm going to finally get his answer. I don't know what I'll do if he says no, but I'm 98% certain that he won't. He was enthralled by the idea when we were in the forest. He *wants* to be my Master. It's almost like he just doesn't realize the subservients have all the control.

The door to the office is closed and the eagle's perch has been moved out onto the landing of the stairs. I don't know if that's a good sign or a bad sign. The familiar nods his head to me and I knock politely. How unlike me.

"Come in."

Lockwood sounds calm. I open the door and step inside.

"You wanted to see me, Sir?" I lean on the word 'sir' for emphasis.

He's standing with his back to me again, staring out over the school like a king overseeing his domain. His hands aren't behind him this time.

"Sit down."

I put my book bag aside and sit in one of the straight-backed chairs that have been provided for guests. I cross my legs and wait, trying to calm my heart rate.

"You've given me quite a lot to think about, Miss Hemlock," he says in a low, calculating voice. "And after much consideration, I have come to the determination that as a Darkblood who has illegally infiltrated my school...."

He turns around, holding a thick bamboo cane in his hand.

My heart skips a beat.

Yes!

"You need to be punished for that infraction."

Oh, I do, Sir. I do.

He swings the cane and strikes his opposite palm, leaving a pink line across his own skin. I flinch at the sound, desperate to feel that sting on my own flesh.

"Stand up."

"Yes, Sir."

I stand primly in front of him, smoothing down my tartan skirt before I hold my hands in front of me. I look up at him through my eyelashes.

"Now what?"

"Now what, *Sir*," he corrects. "That is your last reminder. Turn around and grasp the seat of the chair."

"Yes, Sir."

The chair seat is low enough that when I bend to grasp it, my ass is in the air. He comes forward and kicks my feet out, widening my stance. He yanks my skirt up, revealing my red silk panties. I'm glad those are the ones I wore today. After a moment, his big hands grab the elastic holding the triangles together and slowly pulls them down.

"Step," he orders, and I step out of the panties with one foot. He leaves them around my other ankle.

My palms are sweating and I'm tingling with excitement. He's a strong man, so I expect that he'll hit me hard. I wonder how many strokes he's going to give, and whether he'll say anything.

I bend over again and grasp the seat of the chair firmly.

"Hold still," he orders.

He steps back and I hold my breath. There's a whistling swish, then the cane lands across my naked ass so hard my knees almost buckle. The initial pain isn't that bad, but it intensifies over the seconds that pass until it feels like a thousand wasps are stinging me. I'm just acclimating to that feeling when a second blow lands across the first.

I gasp, my body jerking forward from the force of his strike.

"We do not allow Darkbloods at Everafter," he says, his voice even, but I can hear a little quiver underneath it. I wonder if he's hard already. How I'd love to reach back and find out.

The cane whistles, and another stripe burns into me.

"Dark magic is not allowed here."

Crack.

"Dark witches are not allowed here."

Crack! This blow is harder than the first two. I muffle a whimper.

"You have lied to us."

Crack!

"You lied to *me.*"

CRACK!

This time, I let out a wail as the white-hot pain lances through me. He stops enumerating my sins and just beats me. Blow after blow, the cane sears into my ass and I'm struggling to stay in position. It's getting harder, and my pussy is dripping wet. Tears are falling down my cheeks. Cleansing me. Purifying me for just that little while. I want him to either keep hitting me or put the cane aside and fuck the heaven out of me.

He hesitates and I wave my ass at him, begging for

more, delirious with pain. For a terrifying moment, I think he's going to stop. Then he lays into me and I find myself screaming from the interwoven pain and pleasure. I'm screaming so much that I'm hoarse, my throat burns and I hope all the good little kiddies in the courtyard can hear me.

Lockwood tosses the cane on the floor. It's streaked with blood. *My* blood. I shiver. Then I hear his clothes rustle and I think that the moment I've been waiting for has arrived. One of his big hands rests on my welts and cuts and I hear the wet sound of his hand working his cock. A hot splatter hits my ass and it adds disappointment to my pain. He groans, the sound emotional pain and pleasure combined.

He didn't fuck me. *Damn it. What a waste.*

"Please, Sir," I beg. "I'm so close already. Please..."

"Don't you fucking speak," he grinds out. "This is exactly what you wanted. Pain, depravity and your useless cunt used for my pleasure. Open that mouth again and you'll live to regret it."

I whimper and hang my head. He's right. This is what I wanted.

His cum mixes with my blood and runs down my skin. I start to straighten up, but then his hand is on my back, keeping me down. Two thick fingers push themselves into my slick pussy and he starts ramming them into me at a dizzying pace. I cry out in ecstasy when he curls his fingers and digs them into my G-spot, pushing me over the edge. I cum hard, my insides exploding and the only thing holding me up are his fingers inside me.

He none-too-gently yanks them out, steps away and murmurs a magical command. The prickle of magic courses over my body and the pain eases just a little. The sticky feeling of his cum fades, much to my disappointment.

"Stand up," he commands. "Fix your clothing."

His voice is quiet now. I pull up my panties. The welts on my buttocks have been healed, but only part way, which makes me happy. Now I can keep feeling them for a little while longer.

Lockwood is doing up his trousers and stowing something in one of his desk drawers. He's cleaned himself up with his spell too and the smell of sex has even been taken out of the air. Disappointing. I guess he's got to cover up his tracks.

He won't look at me. "You don't belong here. You will go to Nevermore, effective immediately."

I object profusely. "I *need* to stay here. You don't understand."

"I understand plenty, Miss Hemlock." He's all business now, cold as ice, but I know men. I know he's just hiding, afraid of what he's just done to his student.

"Why? Are you making me leave because you enjoyed what you just did to me?"

His eyes swivel toward me. "You are enrolled as a student here and you cannot be. Full stop."

"No. That's not it." I advance on him and he backs away a step, just like before. "When you kissed me in the forest, you wanted me. You *still* want me. After this, you can't say that you don't." I go for the jugular. "It's bad enough that you're a coward. Don't be a liar, too."

He glares at me ferociously. A part of me thinks he's going to raise a hand to me in anger. He gets a grip at the last possible moment and growls, "I have already given you my decision. You are leaving Everafter. End of discussion."

I sigh, but this has actually played out the way Lucifer said it would.

"Go into your top filing cabinet. My lord left you a present there. I didn't want to do this, but you're leaving me no choice."

Lockwood looks at me suspiciously, but he goes to the cabinet. Inside, he finds a crystal ball, one that fits nicely into the palm of his hand. As soon as he touches it, an image springs to life.

It shows him and me in this very office, but the scene is something that never happened. The clip shows him fucking the daylights out of me, calling me his fucktoy, his little whore, filling my needy cunt. He's choking me and pulling my hair, and I cry out - like I'd make a fuss over something that small. He tells me that I'm his slave and that if I ever tell anybody that he's fucking me, he'll make sure I never graduate and send me away.

Gross misconduct. Abuse of power. Sexual harassment. This is enough to ruin him forever.

Of course, this scene never really happened. It's in a recording crystal, and my Dark Lord made it himself so I know it's seamless. That's what we did last night at the altar, acting out this little scenario. The Prince of Lies knows his job. He told me this would happen and that Lockwood would have no choice but to let me graduate here. I didn't *want* to blackmail him but he brought this on himself.

And it when it comes down to it, I am a villain. This is in my nature.

"I have a duplicate of that in my possession," I explain calmly, "and I can get copies any time I want them. Multiple copies. Enough for the whole High Council, if need be."

He snaps his head toward me, the look of murder on his face. *"What do you want?"*

"To stay here at Everafter. To graduate, no matter what and to be allowed out after curfew whenever I want."

It must be hard for a man who usually runs the show to find out that he's been outmaneuvered. He's the predator trapped by the prey. The scene plays on and he watches. Lockwood's face gets redder and redder, but I can tell he's not completely angry - he's aroused by what he's seeing.

Monkey see, monkey want to do.

The image stops playing and he throws the crystal against the wall. Nice try. No recording crystal is breakable by normal physical means. If he wasn't so pissed off he'd remember that.

I cross my arms. "So... what's it going to be, *coward?*"

He trains his eyes on me, malice flashing in those sapphire depths. "Come back at the Witching Hour and find out." He seizes the cane off the floor and shoves it into the cabinet. "Now get out of my office."

I gather up my books and slip out past the eagle. I can feel it glaring at me all the way down the stairs. I do hope that, once he's cooled down, Lockwood appreciates me leaving my panties for him.

Chapter Nineteen

Ravyn

If I'm honest, I feel a little bad about what I've done to Lockwood. He's only trying to do the right thing. He just doesn't understand. I *can't* leave Everafter. Not only will leaving prevent me from avenging my family, it will send me to hell sooner rather than later. I want to take as much time as possible here. The whole four years, or longer if I can manage it. I still have a life to live and things I want to see before I'm consigned to the Pit forever.

It's possible, but not likely, that Lockwood might actually send me away anyhow. I don't think he will, because if he does, that crystal will cost him his job and possibly his life, depending on Queen Laurette's mood. She's the ruler of Fantasia, the kingdom that hosts Everafter, and even I know she has a very dim view of men who take advantage of innocent young girls. I don't think I've ever been an innocent; but the crystal makes it look like I am and if it comes down to it, I can play the part. Maybe not well, as my tenure here as shown, but I can play it.

Lockwood has too much to lose to call my bluff.

Speaking of bluffs, my thoughts turn to Aladdin. He's a

pretty boy, all right, but I'm convinced he's nothing but a big fat liar. If he does have the goods on people though, he might be a contact worth cultivating. Since it looks like class has ended, I decide to seek him out and see what he has to say. I could do with another distraction anyway.

My entire body is aching with pain, which I love because it dulls the impurity of my soul and all that. It's also making it difficult to walk normally and not hiss whenever I irritate the wounds, so I use a little magic to heal my back and ass. It's not enough to erase the marks, but enough to help me walk like I haven't shit myself.

After many failed attempts trying to find Aladdin on my own, I ask a group of seniors lounging in the courtyard. None of them seem eager to talk to me. They must have heard of all the chaos I've been creating. I can hardly blame them for their reluctance. They don't want to be seen talking to an outcast troublemaker.

As I step back into the school, one of the seniors runs up to me and suggests I check out the groundskeeper's shack at the southern gate. I thank him and walk back through the courtyard toward the gate.

The shack is small and wooden with little circular windows. I really hope this isn't Quasi's home. It's barely fit for a dog kennel. I find Aladdin just outside, wrestling with a bag of grass seed.

He looks up at me and grins. "Hey, if it isn't the prettiest witch in town!"

I smile at the compliment and stroll over to him. "Can we talk... in private?"

His eyebrows shoot up toward his unruly dark hair, and after a moment, he says, "Sure. Come on into my office."

He leads the way into the back of the shack. It's full of bags of grass seed, gardening tools, three wheelbarrows and a stack of bagged peat that makes the whole place smell earthy and wholesome. It's unnerving. Aladdin grins at me and flops down on the bags of peat, which have been arranged in the shape of a chair.

"Just make yourself comfortable" he tells me, sweeping a hand around. "I don't charge visitors."

I sit down gingerly on a rickety wooden stool beside a bench that's full of botanical potions like fertilizers and bug sprays. He watches me, his black eyes studious.

"I wanted to talk to you about what you said in the library, about having secrets."

He puffs. "I do. I have secrets on almost everybody." He winks at me. "I'm a spy by profession, you see."

"Uh-huh. Sure. No real spy is ever going to say, `Hi, I'm a spy.' That's not how this works."

"I *am* a spy," he defends.

"Just not a very good one, it seems?"

He crosses his arms. "For your information, I was hired by the Penny Royal Pack to keep an eye out for Darkbloods. If I see any, I'm supposed to report back so they can bring their hunters here. I won't tell them about you... *if* you help me."

I snort. The Penny Royal Pack are a complete joke. They can barely hunt their own tails. He's either the worst spy in the business or an idiot. He's certainly shit at blackmail. Either way, it might be fun to play along.

"What makes you think I care if you tell them?"

His arms fall down by his side. "Come on. You were totally infringing on my moves with Beauty earlier."

"Moves? Pah. Please. I nearly got off my seat to whoop your sorry ass."

Starry-eyed glee lights up his face. "I would've loved that."

"Masochist?" I ask, curious now.

"Yeah. You?"

"Yeah."

There's a moment of silence, as one masochist sits in front of another. Then we burst out laughing. He's surprisingly funny. I can see why Beauty didn't suckerpunch him when he refused to go away.

"All joking aside," Aladdin continues, folding his arms again, "you came here for a reason. I'm not gonna budge unless you help *me*."

I sigh. "All right, I'll bite. What do you want?"

I'm not prepared for the way he seems to change. His cocksure attitude melts away and I find myself looking into the eyes of a sad little boy.

"I need you to help me find my dad."

His words catch me off guard and I feel a sharp pang of sympathy. I've never felt this for a stranger before and I don't really know how to handle it. When did I turn into a softie?

Stupid white magic.

I keep my voice low. "What happened to him?"

Aladdin sighs and looks away. He pulls up his knees and wraps his arms around them, the long fingers of his right hand gripping his left wrist. He starts to talk in an equally low voice, as if he's afraid someone will hear.

"When I was six years old, my dad, Ali - who was a thief, I'll admit - ran afoul of a Genie when he was on a job." He looks up at me and does air quotes. "'A job,' you know?"

I'm surprised. "He was trying to rob a Genie?"

"More likely the Genie's master." He sighs. "The Genie came to our house and grabbed me and my dad, and he..."

He trails off and I see dark shadows in his eyes.

"He kept my dad, but after a while, he got bored with me and threw me out. He still has my dad."

I feel terrible for him and though he doesn't know it, I understand what it feels like to have your loved ones taken from you.

Aladdin continues, his tone slightly louder but sombre. "I thought the Genie might have been at Nevermore, so I was going to look there and that's where I met the Penny Royal Pack. But then I heard that he's the familiar of a princess named Aaliyah."

That name is a new one to me. "Who's Aaliyah?"

"She's one of the princesses here, but I honestly don't know which one. I think she's in disguise." He looks up at me hopefully. "And that's where you come in. I need you to help me find her."

I ponder it for a moment. It's not like it'll be a hard since disguises are made of enchantments and that's my jam. I can see through most disguises without too much effort at all. I might also be able to use a Genie, if I can get his lamp away from her.

I nod at him. "Okay." An impish thought occurs to me, and I decide to push him to see how far he'll go. "So...you know I'm Darkblood, right?"

He laughs. "At this point, everybody knows that!"

"And do you know how Darkblood seal our deals?"

Aladdin starts to look nervous. "No..."

"We fuck."

I knew the look on his face would be priceless. He looks like he's about to swallow his tongue.

"You... f-fu...?" he squeaks out, his face turning scarlet.

"We fuck," I repeat. "Hard. Do you think you're up to the task?"

My mind gets flooded with images of me saying these

exact words to Lockwood while Broin stands behind me, stroking my body. I have to shake my head to get rid of the thought.

That came out of nowhere.

Aladdin gives me a queasy smile. "Uh... okay. Except I... uh... Well, I haven't..."

My mouth drops open. "You haven't? Not ever?" He shakes his head. "How old are you?"

He blushes deeper, the tinge now purple. "That's got nothing to do with it."

"In Draoich, it's rare to find anybody over fourteen who's a virgin."

He's offended and embarrassed. "Well, I'm — I'm not from Draoich," he blurts out, choking on the words.

"Obviously."

"I'm from Wysteria. Things are different in the mountains."

I struggle not to giggle at him. Honestly, I have no intention of fucking Aladdin. He's already clearly and very hopelessly in love with Beauty.

"Then what do you propose we do?"

He looks around, checking to see if we're alone. In the shack. Really, now? "What about a kiss?"

"If you even say the words true love, rest assured I will throat punch you."

"No, I just... kissing is good. I can do that. We can seal it that way?"

I don't answer him immediately; he's too much fun to mess with.

Instead I cross the distance between us, reach out slowly and touch his face. "No."

"No? What do you mean *no*?" The horrified look on his face is priceless.

I chuckle, then take the matter seriously. While we don't need to fuck non-Satanists in order to seal a deal, there does need to be some kind of physical contact. A handshake, a high five, a kiss on the cheek or lips. That sort of thing. I'm very tempted to kiss Aladdin the Satanic way, but I don't want to scare him.

I kneel in front of him, my face just inches from his. His eyes are wide and fixed on my own. I can hear his heart beating in his chest, frantic and terrified and it's a beautiful sound to me.

Leaning forward, I bring my lips to his mouth, hover there for a moment...teasing him, torturing him...then I peck him on the cheek. When I pull back, Aladdin is holding his breath, his shoulders tensed and his face an unnatural shade of plum.

I straighten off the floor, dusting my hands on my skirt. "Now that's out of the way, it's time to seal the deal."

"B-but you just said—"

"What, that? I was just playing with you. To actually seal this we'll need a headless chicken, two pregnant goats, a ram's testicle and the blood of a virgin. I don't suppose you have those ingredients to hand, do you?"

Aladdin looks at me as if I've just grown an extra head. "You're not all there, are you?"

Walking out of the shack door, I grin over my shoulder at him. "No, but don't worry, if I was this deal would never have been made. See you on the flipside, baby."

Chapter Twenty

Ravyn

Later that night, with the waxing moon high in the inky-black sky, I get ready for my rendezvous with Lockwood. I take one last look in the bathroom mirror. My complexion is glowing, visible to other witches like me, because our powers are stronger at the Witching Hour. As is customary at this time of night, I'm wearing my velvet crimson cloak, draped over my naked body.

Thankfully, Alice is asleep. Her light snores make me smile as I head for the door, wondering where Sirena is. I haven't seen her since dinner.

Broin caws at me from the windowsill, and I look over my shoulder at him.

—*What's wrong?*—

—*Be careful,*— he warns.

—*This is part of the Dark Lord's plan, remember?*—

His head twitches to the side. —*Yes, but we still don't know if we can trust this Lockwood fully.*—

Touched by his concern, I go over and press a kiss to his little head.

—*It's Witching Hour. I'll be okay.*— Stroking the length of his back, I suggest, —*Why don't you come with me? I'm sure he won't notice you watching through the window and I'm sure you'll enjoy the view. What do you say, Daddy?*—

He shakes his head and ruffles his feathers. I know he doesn't want me to go, yet he understands why I must. I need this, not just because Lucifer ordered me to, but because the Dark Witch within me craves to be in pain whenever she can. Broin isn't able to give me that as often as I need it without my roommates getting suspicious. I don't want the girls to find out my familiar is also a man. I adore them more than I thought I would, but I'm not sure how they'll react. The thought of losing Broin...

—*Go have fun, Little Red, but be wary.*—

—*Aren't I always?*— I smile and lift my hood over my head. —*Don't worry about me. I've got everything under control... I think.*—

—*You'd better.*—

He lowers his beak and watches me leave the room.

I gently close the door and look around the hallway. It's empty and I don't see Mrs. Thornhart prowling around. Just to be on the safe side, I cast a glamour anyway and just manage to stifle my sneeze.

I gingerly climb down the stairs into the common room. My feet root to the spot when I find Sirena curled up on the balcony. Her face is pressed against the misted glass and tear stains mark her cheek. I almost want to remove the veil and and ask whose ass I need to kick, but then someone comes down from the boy's dormitories and calls out her name.

"Sirena, baby. I'm sorry."

It's Erik. Ew.

A quick glance at the clock reminds me that Witching Hour is in exactly ten minutes. I'm already running late. I leave the common room, making a mental note to find her at breakfast. If I find out Erik has hurt her again, a bitch will die.

The following hallway is also empty. The lanterns flicker as I walk by and I climb down the stairs and head toward the Great Hall. I hold my breath as I creep by the entrance, catching a glimpse of Mrs. Thornhart talking to Quasi. She turns her head toward the door, ever so slightly and I swear it's like she saw me. I scurry down the hallway, hoping to Satan I'm not being followed.

I climb the tower stairs leading to his office, my stomach fluttering with nervous excitement. I think about how cruel Lockwood's voice had been, how calculating his touch, how beautifully villainous he was when he punished me. My body tingles from the memory, my ass still raw from his cane. At that moment, he wasn't my headmaster; he was a man intent on taking his revenge out on my body and I loved every second of it. I know he loved it too. The jizz he'd shot onto my ass was concrete evidence.

By the time I reach his door, Lockwood is already waiting on me. I gulp and stare up at his body swallowing up the doorway. He looks positively enraged, which sends a thrill of excitement through me. It's the first time I've seen him without his robes or suit coat. His white shirt, unbuttoned at the neck, strains as he folds his arms and glares at me.

"You're late, witch."

Not Redera or Miss Hemlock.

Witch.

He narrows his eyes into cutting slits and a chill runs down my spine. "I'm sorry, Sir."

"What was that?" One of his eyebrows lifts up, ducking

underneath loose strands of hair. "I'm sure you can do better than that, girl."

My cheeks flare and I gaze up at him. He must want me to call him Daddy or Master. Since Broin is already my Daddy and always will be, I choose the latter. "I'm sorry for being late, Master Lockwood."

Headmaster and student, Master and slave. Such a perfect turn of events.

Lockwood nods his head. "Get in."

Stepping back but still holding the door, he watches me slide by his familiar and into the room. The furniture is all the same except where his desk is. A wooden cross stands in front of it. The piece of equipment is the length of my body and draped over the side is a cat'o'nine tails.

My heart rate spirals, banging against my ribcage like wild pistons. It's been nearly three months since I've felt the kiss of that particular whip. His Excellency flagellated me at the last Satanalia. I touch the side of my neck, where the scars crown my skin. He had once whipped parts of me so severely that no magic or spell could heal. It was his gift to me for my sixteenth birthday.

"Do you like the look of that, girl?" Lockwood whispers by ear.

"Yes," I breathe out, shuddering at his words.

His seizes my throat from behind, his grip capturing me like a vice. Brushing my hair over one shoulder, he slides his palm down my body and around my front. A gust of cool air caresses my skin as he pulls my cloak to the side and exposes my pussy. His fingers glide over my lower lips, teasing me.

"Already wet and I haven't even started. Does the thought of being whipped by your headmaster make you quiver, witch?"

I hold my breath, nodding my reply.

"You really are a Darkblood," he scoffs, pulling his fingers back. "Get on that cross. And don't keep me waiting."

Tentatively, I approach and face the wooden frame, waiting for him to strap me down.

"Uh-uh." He clicks his tongue. "The other way. Your tits and cunt are mine tonight. I want to see them."

I turn around, gently press my back to the wood and watch him. He's picking something off his desk. When he turns back around, he's holding a riding crop and his face is completely wiped clean of emotion. I can't tell at all what he's thinking.

That actually excites me more than the crop.

He prowls over to me with slow, confident strides, snaking the implement through his fingers. Wrapping a strong hand around my waist, he places the crop between his teeth and lifts me up effortlessly. He secures my hands and feet in iron shackles nailed to each of the legs, then removes the crop from his mouth and takes a step back.

I'm completely splayed before him.

A mere object for him to use and fill as he sees fit.

He already knows this, going by the grin playing on his lips.

He walks around the cross, scrutinizing me closely. After a quick once over, he then pivots on his heel and retrieves another object from his desk. He returns with a throng of metal clips, each attached to a thin gold chain. There's at least twenty of them. Twenty clips to inflict pain on my body.

Tonight is going to be one heaven of a night.

Slowly opening one of the clips, he slides me a glance. "You wanted to feel pain. You wanted me to take control of your slut body. You wanted me to treat you like the fucktoy you are."

None of these are questions, but I nod anyway. "Yes, S...Master," I correct my sloppiness. "I do. So, *so* much."

His eyes darken and he snaps the clip shut. "You'll speak when I say you can, witch." Closing the distance between us, he reaches up and unfastens my cloak. The material slips away and puddles at my feet, allowing the air and moonlight to soak my body. "You're under my control now and you're going to obey every single order I give you. Is that understood?"

"Yes, Master."

Lockwood clamps one clip on my left nipple. I gasp at the unexpected sharpness. He only chuckles. The next clip isn't as sore because I know what's coming so I can anticipate it. What I don't anticipate is Lockwood placing the clips in a line across my breasts, then in another from my throat down to my stomach, forming the God of Light's unholy cross.

I have Lucifer's mark on my back and his enemy's on my front.

This will not go down well with him.

Stepping back, Lockwood sweeps his eyes over my body, drinking everything in. My blood gushes into my breasts until they're nothing but two swollen mounds. He pulls the chain at my navel. It's connected to all of the clips and the downward pressure forces them to tighten and pull. The pain is instant and I hiss through clenched teeth, my eyes stinging.

"Here's what's going to happen, witch," Lockwood starts, leisurely rolling up his sleeves one by one, his eyes riveted on my face. "You're going to repeat everything I say, witch, and if you know what's good for you, you'll do *exactly* as you're told. Do you understand?"

The tattoos covering his forearms catch my attention. I knew he had them but I never expected so many. I follow the faint outlines through his shirt and now that I'm properly looking for them, it seems as if they're covering every inch of his body. That is, where his suit can't hide.

He yanks the chain again and I yelp. "I asked you a question. You'd do well to answer."

"Yes, Master. I...I *understand*."

He widens his eyes at my hesitation and disrespectful tone of voice. This time he doesn't just pull the chain, he twists the clip on my nipple until I let out a scream. "Sorry, what was that?"

"*Aargh!*" I arch my back as much as I can against the cross. "I understand, Master. I'll obey you."

He smiles and lightly slaps my cheek. "Good girl." Swiping the crop against his palm, he orders calmly, "Now, repeat after me. I renounce Satan and all his works."

My eyes bulge in their sockets. Is he insane? I can't do that. I already *failed* at trying to do that and look what happened. I bite my tongue, refusing but also unable to answer. My silence receives a sharp flick of his crop.

The leather tongue sails over my breast, jolting every clip, and the pain is sensational. It spreads through my body in viscous waves the more and faster he strikes, flooding my pussy, igniting every inch of desire coursing through my veins.

"Say it, witch."

Another swipe. I yank at my bonds, suppressing my whimpers.

"I renounce Satan." Swipe. "You are no longer my master."

Does he not understand? I can't abandon my god again.

"Say." Swipe. "It." Swipe.

I can't. I can't!

Lockwood's pace is increasing, the pressure on my body breaking skin.

I don't ask him to stop. Pain is all I know. It's all I want.

And right now, he's the one I want to give it to me.

Droplets of sweat trickle down his forehead, his chest heaving with exertion. "How could you possibly want all this pain?" His voice is quiet, losing that sinister edge.

I peek at him through my lashes, my body trembling and bleeding on the cross. "I need this pain as much as you crave to give it, Master. It's in your blood, every last droplet of it, just like it's in mine. We're both the same; You're only just now acknowledging it."

His nostrils flare, his countenance shifting from curious to enraged in a split second. With one ruthless yank, he rips the clips off my body, the pain searing every cell in my body.

He grabs the cat o' nine and snaps it in front of me. "You want pain, witch? Here it fucking is."

Something inside him cracks.

Breaks.

Unleashes.

And he flogs me with an irrepressible fury.

His hatred and lust transmits through his whip into my flesh, his powerful, heaving body nothing more than pure and utter contained strength that could bend me in half.

Strike after strike, my skin breaks and bleeds under the cruelty of his whip. The pain robs me of my vision and I close my eyes, biting my lips to suppress the screams. Blood spurts onto my tongue, the sharp tang polluting my senses. I'm just flesh and bone on this cross now, here for him to mold as he wishes. He could kill me if he wanted to and I'd probably let him because this pain, sweet, glorious pain, is the best sensation in the world.

A light spreads through my veins, basking me in a beautiful, blinding warmth. Moments of purity. Glimmers of goodness. They're so beautiful that I start to cry, wishing the warmth would never end, never leave me in the dark again. Is this what Redera felt? Whole, pure and untainted without having to suffer? Without having to be punished by His Excellency in his Red Dungeon?

Lockwood throws the whip on the floor. I can't lift my head to look at him. All I can hear is his rapid pants and his hands unshackling me. I collapse into his arms, a pile of shredded flesh. My magic is already healing me, though it will take time to complete the task. Until then, I'll savor every painful welt and cut seared into my body. This is exactly what I wanted. Needed. Craved.

In a series of blurs, Lockwood spins me around and shoves me face down into the cross, his cock jabbing my pussy. Just before he enters me, he stops, and it takes me a moment to realize why. He's seeing my back for the first time.

The mark that Lucifer gave me.

The scars that have never really healed from the years of punishments.

He trails his fingers down and over every inch of my back, just like Broin did. He even prods the welts like he did. It's like they're both mesmerised by it. I guess in a sadistic way, it's like artwork.

"Do you really enjoy this?" he asks, his voice low as he traces the nearly healed lines. He sounds almost guilty.

"Yes," I assure him. "I truly love it."

"Why?" His cock nudges me a little.

"Because…it's the only way people like me…can experience pleasure," I manage between pants, my erratic heartbeat making it impossible to catch my breath. "Some of us enjoy inflicting pain. Others, like me, crave it."

He slides into my pussy and I moan, the pain mixing with pleasure. The warmth within me is singing, exploding into a million little stars.

"Go on."

I press my head into the frame, giving me that bit of support to angle my hips correctly. "The God of Light did this to us. When we abandoned him, he forsook our clan and made it so we could only know joy through suffering."

His thrusts start off slow, stretching me to the hilt and then pulling out again. I can feel him throbbing inside me, so I keep talking.

"This is all I've ever known."

"Mm, fuck," he groans, impaling me on his cock.

"That's what makes me a Darkblood. I want pain more than I want pleasure."

He threads a hand through my hair, but instead of yanking back, shoves me into the cross. His thrusts become deeper and harder. Guttural moans build in my throat and escape through my lips. Ecstasy fizzles through my body, starting in my pussy and spreading to every nerve I have.

He's getting close and so am I. My insides clench around his cock and his groans deepen. His grip on my hair tightens. He pulls out and rams into me again.

"Your stupid Storyteller thought this would curse us,

but we grew to love it." Another powerful thrust, lifting me off my feet. "We grew to want it more than anything."

Lockwood pulls out, spins me around, pushes me onto my knees and jerks his cock over my breasts. He gives three swift strokes and then his cum spurts out onto my flayed skin. He barely finishes shaking the head when he pulls me back up to my feet, jams his fingers inside me and ruthlessly assaults my G-spot.

He circles and flicks my clit with his other hand and I'm a goner.

The sensation bursts like a dam inside, gushing out of me and onto the floor. My legs buckle under the pressure. Lockwood holds me up and brings his face to mine. I think he's going to kiss me but he just stares into my eyes, seeking answers to questions I wasn't prepared for him to ask. There's something more than just hunger and lust in his gaze. Something almost tender.

Setting me on the ground, he goes into his drawer and pulls out an ivory wand. The handle is long and curved, the edge shaped like an eagle. The core must be made of wolfsbane, going by the slightly nauseating tinge.

He motions me to come forward. "Let's get those welts seen to."

I shake my head at him, despite the fact that I can barely stand. "I can heal them myself, but where's the fun in that? I like to feel them, Sir. It's the masochist in me."

Every movement is just a painful, glorious reminder of how I received them. Another scar to wear like paint on a canvas.

"You're bleeding," he disputes.

"I know. Isn't it wonderful?"

I grin and turn around so he can see the marks left on my body. Lucifer. Broin. Him. I hear his footsteps coming over. His hot breath tickles the nape of my neck, sending shivers through me. He touches the welt between my shoulder blades and then runs his fingers down the length of my spine, deliberately prodding each mark with dexterous precision.

I shudder under his touch.

He nearly flayed me alive and already I want more.

"How can you worship a god who taught you to cherish such cruelty?"

His words cut through me like his whip did to my flesh.

I turn around and look up at him. "He never taught me to cherish cruelty. I already told you it was the God of Light — your Storyteller — that cursed my clan because we stopped believing in him. And yet he preaches forgiveness."

Lockwood frowns and turns me around by the shoulder. I don't register what he's doing until it's too late. The tingling sensation stretches over my back, through my chest and down to my toes.

"Wait!"

I try to grab his wand but he seizes my wrist with his other hand.

"If we're going to do this," he says, digging his fingers into my skin, "we're doing it my way. I'll give you your pain, Ravyn, but you'll never walk away from me torn to bits. Not under my watch."

Well, fuck me sideways.

It's rare that I'm ever lost for words.

Every wound in my body heals, including my gift from Lucifer. I'm pissed about that but I know the mark will still be there. I'll never be able to get away from it.

"Why do you even care?" I finally ask, turning around

to face him again. "I'm the person forcing you to do all this."

I threatened his life, his career, his reputation just to get what I want. Not that I'm feeling guilty about it anymore. I'm just curious why he doesn't want me to suffer more than I need to.

He pauses for a moment and glances down, contemplating his words carefully. I hold my breath, my heart skittering in anticipation. At last he looks up. "Because I might as well have some fucking fun here."

I'm surprised by the giggle I make. I knew the instant I laid eyes on Lockwood he was like me. I just never knew how much.

Exhausted but content, I look around for my cloak. I move away from Lockwood and approach the cross. Time to go home. I'm beat.

"Where do you think you're going?"

I freeze upon hearing the words. "I thought we were done here?"

Lockwood folds his arms over his chest. "That was just the beginning. You're going to come with me to my private quarters and I'm going to fuck you until the sun rises. Count your blessings tomorrow is a no school day. Now..." He turns to the door behind his desk. "Shall we get started?"

Chapter Twenty-One

Gideon

There's a full moon tonight.

The school locks down when this happens, a legacy of the time when there were wolves outside every gate, howling to come and sink their teeth into some fresh meat. Since wolves have been banished to Draoich, the need to lock down hasn't been as pressing. Or so people like to think.

There are still dark creatures on the full moon, things that roam among the trees, hunting the stupid and the unwary. They only eat one night a month, so they're pretty much ravenous.

I know how that feels.

I got up late today, our free day, because I spent too much time last night with Christopher. His familiar is an owl and he's getting just as nocturnal as his bird. That means that I don't get to sleep at a reasonable time, because he's my stinking roommate. Up at all hours, banging around in the room, talking to his bird out loud when he should be able to do it in his head... he's annoying. I tell him so, and he tries to shape up, but he backslides.

Last night was a big backslide. Not that I minded that much.

Today, though, like I always do when I get laid the night before, I overslept and missed breakfast. And lunch. And also dinner. The cafeteria will be closed until morning, so I've got nothing to do but drag my hangry ass around the courtyard looking for people to talk to.

I pass a bunch of girls in the last rays of daylight, making signs for the big Samhain Masqued Ball. Typical committee girls and they don't disappoint. When I walk by, they lose track of what they're doing and stare at me. My ass is looking particularly fetching in my tight trousers today, if I say so myself, and I know they'd all love a piece of me. I wink at them and the littlest one giggles into her hand, overcome by my animal magnetism.

Heh.

Too easy.

Up ahead, in our usual spot under the dryad oak, my friends are already hanging around. Cinder is sitting on a blanket with a parasol held over her head, probably afraid something will drop on her. Her hands are in the white gloves she wears to hide the fact that she washes them until they're raw and they're busy twirling the parasol. She looks to be listening with great seriousness to whatever Erik is jawing about. Christopher is sitting on her other side, his back against the tree, nodding sagely, a book in his lap.

Fang trots up to me. He's been my familiar for five years, and I honestly would be lost without him. He's the only thing I loved back home, and now home is anywhere he is. He wags his tail at me and reports, —*I didn't see the Darkblood.*—

I nod. —*She's probably out gathering toadstools or*

something.—

—Or something.—

Aurora is lying on the blanket next to Cinder, her head propped up on her hand. Her other arm is lying on top of her hip and it draws my eyes to the curve of her body. She's got a nice, tight little hourglass and I've been working on finding out if her pussy is the same. So far she hasn't given in, but I suspect that the Masque is when it'll happen. She looks up at me and smiles and her lips are so petal-pink that it sort of distracts me. Aurora's got a cup of coffee sitting in front of her and she dips a finger inside it. Her blue eyes looking up at me, she sticks that finger in her mouth and gives it a nice long suck.

Oh, yeah.

That's gonna be my dick in that little mouth one of these days.

The mental image of getting blown by Aurora doesn't stay for long. Truth be told, there's someone much sexier in school and I'd die happy if she were to take my cock between her lips. Fat chance I'd ever admit it, though. Decent princes don't want to get sucked off by a Darkblood witch.

Rapunzel looks up as Fang and I approach. "Finally! We're all here. Now we can get down to business."

I sit down beside Aurora and lean back on my hands. "What business?"

Erik answers bitterly, "The Darkblood. We have to get rid of her."

"Agreed. How do you propose that we do it? Just stick her on a broomstick and fly her out of here?"

Aurora laughs and playfully shoves my shoulder. "You're always so funny, Gid!"

I blow her a kiss and give a wink. She nearly chokes on

her coffee when she takes a sip. Wish she could be choking on something else.

Rapunzel muses, "The Samhain Masque is coming up. What if we enchant her mask to stick to her face, but when she takes it off, it takes off all of her skin, too?"

"Ew!" Cinder objects. "That's so... Draoich."

"I'm trying to fight fire with fire." She holds onto her precious hair, terrified they'll turn into snakes again.

I laugh. "You'd better think of something else, Punzi, because your enchantments don't do diddly squat to her."

Erik glares. "Fucking witch."

"Not that I disagree," I say, as Fang lies down beside me, "but what did she do to you that makes you so mad at her today?"

"It's Sirena," he answers. "She's making her think all kinds of stupid things."

"Like what kind of things?" Christopher asks quietly.

"Like maybe she doesn't need a prince because Redera doesn't have one, and she's so *cool*."

I roll my eyes. "As if. No prince would want her."

"Probably would make your dick..." Erik begins, but he bites it back. "Sorry, ladies."

Aurora gives him a displeased squint. "Don't be vulgar. You're a prince not an animal."

"Sorry." He gives her an apologetic smile and she brushes his hand with hers like she's giving him something special.

"All is forgiven," she says, sounding so much like her mother Lauretta that I can't stand it.

"See what the Darkblood's doing?" Punzi says, her voice strident. "She's bringing out the worst in all of us."

"To be honest, Erik can be pretty vulgar anyway," Chris states.

She ignores him. Of all of us, she knows how obscene Erik can sometimes be. He's her boyfriend, after all. Sometimes. She goes on. "I'm serious. Just by having her here, she's polluting all of Everafter. Who knows what kind of horrible things a dark witch can inspire in people? All of our darkness is going to be put on show and we're not supposed to have darkness!"

I look at Chris and roll my eyes. His sister has always been melodramatic. I remember at her fifth birthday when Chris ate the frosting flower off her piece of cake. You'd have thought he'd slit her throat... and she still hasn't totally forgiven him.

"I don't think that's fair," Chris argues in his quiet voice. He looks at me for back-up, his green eyes soft and pleading. I like that look on his face when we're alone, but here it just winds me up.

"Why not?" Aurora asks. "We were all fine, just fine, until *she* showed up."

Cinder nods. "I agree. She's a bad influence. She has to go."

I lie back and pull Fang into a loose cuddle. His white fur goes up my nose, and I sneeze, which makes Chris laugh. He looks into my eyes with a little smile and I can't help but remember some of the finer moments from last night. He'd looked fucking amazing writhing underneath me.

"We need to get together with our magic and do something at the Masque that will completely humiliate her," Punzi says, glaring daggers into an ant that's walking across the blanket.

"Don't frown," Aurora warns. "You'll get wrinkles."

"How do you humiliate a witch?" Erik wonders. "Do they even have emotions?"

"Yes," Punzi nods. "They have hatred and spite and malice and..."

"All of the things you're displaying right now."

We all gape at Christopher.

"Are you on her side?" Aurora demands. "After everything she's done? After my makeup? After Rapunzel's *hair*?"

I snicker. "You have to admit, that was kind of hilarious."

Punzi rubs at her face where the snakes bit her. "No, it most certainly was not."

"No, it wasn't," my roommate agrees. "It was mean. But so is what you're planning on doing to her. You know she wouldn't be here if she were totally evil, right?"

"I don't care." I shrug at him. "She's a Darkblood. And I hate Darkbloods."

Chris looks at me with so much disappointment that I have to look away. "You're a bigot," he declares.

My mouth falls open. He's never criticized me in anything before. Why the hell is he starting now? Maybe Punzi is right, the witch *is* bringing out the worst in us. Chris has never opposed me before and I don't like it.

"Listen, you bleeding heart little asshole," I start, glaring at him. He lowers his head. "You'd better decide which side you're on. Are you with us, the students who belong here at Everafter, or are you going to be with that Draoich bitch who somehow got in here?"

His head still bent, he mutters, "I just think she's nicer than you think she is."

Punzi laughs sharply. "Nice? Are you *kidding*?"

"She was kind to Quasi."

She shakes her head in confusion. "Who's that?"

"The gardener."

Cinder looks surprised. "I didn't think it had a name."

"He. *He* has a name," Chris corrects, raising his voice.

I roll my eyes. "Whatever. He's just a deformed peasant. Why do we care if she's nice to him? That's just like attracting like. He digs in the dirt, she *is* dirt…"

The look Chris gives me is full of disapproval and I'll be honest, it stings. But I don't show it.

He mumbles again, "I just don't think you're being fair, is all."

"Fair," Aurora mimics snidely. "Do you think she'll care about fairness when she takes everything she learns here and uses it against us in the next Silva War?"

Chris rolls his eyes, a habit he picked up from me when we were kids. "There's not going to be a next Silva War."

"You don't know that," she challenges. "Worse, if there is, you're going to be a traitor to your own kind if you keep this up."

To my amazement and annoyance, Chris stands up. "I might be a traitor, but at least I have a conscience."

He turns and walks away, and I'm filled with unreasonable fear that he's leaving us. He's leaving *me*. I feel like I've been stabbed in the gut.

"That little fuckhead," I growl, schooling my features. "Can you believe this shit?"

Erik shakes his head. "I never thought I'd live to see the day…."

Aurora sits up and watches him leave with a shocked expression on her face. She and Chris are betrothed, not that it means anything to either of them right now. She's horrified at the idea of spending the rest of her life to a witch-lover.

I watch my roommate walk away and I feel pretty much the same thing.

Chapter Twenty-Two

Christopher

I wish I could say that I'm surprised by the things my friends are saying, but I'm not. I've known all of them for too long. They're great when you're part of the group, but if you're on the outside? Even a fairy godmother couldn't save you.

I'm so disappointed in Gideon. This isn't who he really is, not deep down inside. I know him better than anybody else and I know he's not a bad person. Not really. He's just afraid he's never going to measure up, so he tries to be the biggest, meanest dude around so nobody questions him. He has a lot of secrets and he's so afraid of anybody finding out. So what does he do? He finds someone else with secrets of her own and he gets his friends wound up to crap all over her.

It isn't fair. And damn it, I care about fairness.

In my kingdom people aren't shunned for being different. In fact, differences are celebrated. We're a land of honour and integrity and that's a combination that makes you see things clearly. I don't know why someone with dark blood who does good things should be shunned.

Redera was born Darkblood. Everybody can see that.

It must be hard for her to go against her nature, to be nice to people like Quasi and Alice when the rest of the school sort of kicks them all the time. I saw her being kind to him when she didn't have to be and that counts for a lot. I mean, we're all so sweet and mild that butter wouldn't melt in our mouths when Lockwood is around, but that's just because we're being watched. Most of us don't stay so nice when there's not an audience. Redera doesn't care if people are watching, though. She is who she is, all the time.

More or less. Like I said, she has secrets, too.

Right now, I have a secret that she needs to know. I need to find her to warn her about what my friends are planning.

Everafter loves balls. We have one every season. Everybody who's anybody anywhere in the Great Forest shows up for the Everafter balls, especially for the Samhain Masque. It's the biggest of big deals and for the girls to be plotting how to humiliate Redera at a function like this, well... that's just mean.

I go into the main building and hesitate at the base of the stairs to the girls' dormitories. It's a punishable offense for a prince to be caught in a princess's chambers, as I learned to my sorrow the first day I was here at Everafter. Professor Lockwood is a very serious customer and boy, can he wield a cane. That day stands out in my head in big, bold, red letters and I'm not in any hurry to repeat it.

I've got to see if Redera is in her room and there's only one way to do that. I have to go up. I look around for any sign of Thornhart and when the coast is clear, I scurry up the stairs to the Odd Box.

That's what we call their room. The Odd Box. All three of the girls who stay there are kind of outcasts, weird in their own way and so it was kismet that they ended up rooming together. I know of a few other girls who had space for another roommate, but I think nobody but Sirena and Alice could have met Redera Hemlock and not been frightened of her. Honestly? I'm glad they found each other. Everybody needs friends, because life sucks when you're alone.

I knock on the door. There's no sound inside and after a minute I turn around to leave. Before I get more than two steps away, the door opens and Alice Underland is standing there with her big rabbit in her arms. She stares at me, her big eyes forever wide and unmoving. That look of hers is a little disconcerting to a lot of people, but I think I can understand it. Who hasn't seen a few things they'd rather forget?

"Can I help you?" she asks. Her voice is whispery and soft.

I crane my neck so I can see around her. The crow's cage is empty. "Is Redera around?"

"No."

"Do you know where she is?"

Alice shakes her head. Her pixie-cut black hair shines and sways like silk in the breeze.

"No," she says. Her innocent eyes turn wary. "Why do you want to know?"

I sigh and explain to her, "I need to tell her something. Something important."

She raises an eyebrow. "I don't think anything you or your friends have to say is important to her." She starts to shut the door in my face. I catch it with an outstretched hand.

"Please...I'm trying to help."

Alice steps aside. "Come in, then, before somebody sees you."

I walk into the room and she closes the door behind me. The room smells like girls, their perfume and their shower gel and I'm sort of out of my element. I shift on my feet nervously. Alice sits down with her rabbit and watches me.

"I... I came to warn her."

"About what?"

"About Aurora and her friends."

She turns her head slightly and squints an eye at me. "I thought they were your friends, too."

"They are," I admit, "but that doesn't mean I like everything they do. They're going to try to run Redera out of Everafter."

Alice sighs and rolls her eyes. "Is that all? That's not news."

I've had about enough of being dismissed for one lifetime.

"Look, I know I've done nothing to make you think that you can trust me, but I swear, you totally can. Okay? Aurora, Rapunzel, Erik, Cinder and Gideon are all going to use their magic to make her look bad at the Samhain Masqued Ball. I don't know how far they're going to go - if they're just going to do something embarrassing, or if they're going to do something to hurt her. And I wanted to warn her before either of that happens."

She sits and strokes her rabbit for a moment, her eyes so unfocused I wonder if she's heard a word I've said. Finally, she replies, "I'm not strong enough to counterspell that many people."

"No. Me, neither." I think fast. "So maybe we can counterspell it before it's a spell, you know?"

Alice stares at me. "I have no idea what you're talking about."

"I mean, do something that will prevent them from casting anything. Like this stuff I heard of... back in Aira, my father's ministers make anybody coming in for a private audience take a pinch of this stuff. It's a powder that suppresses a magic user's abilities so they're just... normal."

"Permanently?"

"No. It's just temporary."

She listens, then says, "Do you, like you know, have some?"

That's where the complications start. "Well, no."

"Do you know where you can get it?"

The look on her face is so doubtful that I want to try twice as hard to prove myself to her. "No, but I'll bet I know someone who does."

WE GO TO THE GROUNDSKEEPER'S HOUSE, DOWN IN THE garden that Quasi tends. I can tell that Alice has never been here, but I ended up here on day one after I got completely blitzed on hard cider in the wine cellar and got lost trying to get back to my room. I still don't know how I ended up here, but I remember it.

Aladdin is always bragging about knowing secrets about everyone, but the truth is he's an inveterate thief. He learned from his father, Ali. Of course, Aladdin is probably a better criminal than his old man was, because to my knowledge, Aladdin has never been arrested - unlike his old man, who spent a few years with forty of his best friends in Wysteria's dungeon. Aladdin is a rotten spy, but his reputation says that when it comes to stealing things and working the black market, there's nobody better.

"Aladdin?" I call out. "Quasimodo?"

I lead the way and Alice follows me closely, clutching her familiar to her chest like she's afraid. I don't know, maybe she has a bad history with plants. You never know what happens in people's lives.

The door to the greenhouse is closed, which seems strange. Quasi has never had this door shut any of the times I've come down here. Not that I come down here all the time. Like, three, maybe four times. Once every day I've been here. That's all. That's not a lot. I just... like the flowers, and the quiet.

I put my hand on the doorknob, but I feel like I'm trespassing, so instead of opening up, I call out again, "Aladdin? Quasimodo?"

There's no answer. I turn the knob.

The greenhouse is awfully dark. The stained glass window that adorns the back wall is covered in a thick black drape, like someone is trying to either hide or protect it.

I hear Aladdin before I see him. "Get out of here."

I stop short, because he's never rude like this. He's always friendly and welcoming. "Aladdin? Is that you?"

I hear him scramble under one of the potting tables, and there's a metallic *clank*. "Go away. Please."

Alice and I look at each other, then we hurriedly move farther into the glass-walled building. We find Aladdin in the nude, wearing a thick leather collar that's chained to a heavy iron ring inset in the stone pathway. Alice gasps and I know my eyes about fall out of my head. He tries to cover his nakedness with his hands, looking away in embarrassment.

"You weren't supposed to find me," he says miserably. "Quasi promised nobody would look here."

"What the hell is going on here?" I demand, hoping no one imprisoned him here.

"Nothing."

Alice frowns. "It doesn't look like nothing. We've got to get you out of here."

"NO!"

The vehemence of Aladdin's shout takes us both by surprise and Alice shrinks back a little. He catches himself and speaks again in a more controlled tone.

"You can't unchain me. It isn't safe."

"What are you talking about?" It's Alice who voices this before I can.

He closes his eyes and comes out from under the table. "You can't unchain me, because this is the only way I won't hurt people tonight."

Tonight is the full moon. There's only one reason an otherwise nice guy would worry about hurting people on full moon night.

Alice vocalizes the question, again beating me to it. "Are you... a wolf?"

It can't be. Wolves have been expunged from the Western Wood for generations. They're dangerous, evil creatures, the sort of thing that parents use to frighten their children into behaving. They're terrifying and I can't believe that he's been here all along. How can a wolf hide in Everafter? How could a Darkblood like Redera get in, too? Lockwood isn't keeping a very good watch... unless he's dark, too. My brain starts to spin with conspiracy theories and I try not to get carried away by my imagination. One thing at a time.

Aladdin hangs his head in shame. "I was cursed. The

Genie who kidnapped my father and me put this curse on me before he dumped me on the street. If I'm not kept in here, chained like this, I'm dangerous. Too dangerous."

We stare at him in shock and he stands and covers himself with his hands.

"Have you killed people before?" I ask softly, genuinely praying the answer is no.

Aladdin closes his eyes. "Yes. That's why *this...*" He shakes the chain. "... has to happen."

My pretty companion shakes her head. "I don't approve, but I think I understand. But... no. Different question. Have you seen Red?"

He nods. "I saw her after dinner. She went out hunting with her familiar."

Alice turns on her heel and starts to march out. I grab her arm. "Hold on. Where do you think you're going?"

"I'm going to find her."

I shake my head. "No. You can't go out there. It's nearly dark and there are *things* hunting out there."

She whirls to face me and her normally pale face is flushed. "Yes, but my friend is out there..."

"She knew the chance she was taking." I sigh. "She's a witch. If anyone would know what the full moon brings, it would be her. She can handle herself."

Alice is frustrated, I can tell and very worried about Red. I'm worried about her, too, but I know better than to go clumping around out in the bush when things much more suited to that environment than I am are ready to eat me. She bends her head down and stares at the floor.

Aladdin speaks again. His voice sounds gravelly and strange. "I need you both to leave now."

Quasi comes into the greenhouse now with a blanket

and a bowl of water. He looks surprised to see us standing there, and his eyebrows rise.

"Sorry," I tell him, not knowing for sure if he can hear or understand me. "We were looking for Redera."

Alice's head snaps up and she says, "I know what to do. Come with me."

We leave the greenhouse at speed and it's all I can do to keep up with her. She moves awfully fast. She's practically running, taking steps two at a time.

I struggle to stay with her. "Where are you going?"

She pulls me out of the stairwell and into one side hall, then another. Soon we're in front of a closet where the extra teaching supplies are stored. Alice grabs the doorknob and faces me.

"I can reach her without going out into the forest," she explains, "and if you tell anybody I can do this, I will pull your liver out through your ear."

I blink. "That sounds deeply unpleasant."

She studies my face for a moment, then says, "I'm trusting you, Christopher."

"I'm honored," I say and it's true. I am. Trust is more precious than gold. "What do you need me to do?"

Alice leads the way into the closet and from there through a door that opens onto a tiny bedroom. There's a narrow bed, barely big enough for a grown man and an enchanted candle whose eternal flame casts golden shadows around the room. She sits on the bed with her rabbit in her lap.

"I have a skill," she says slowly. "A special gift. Or a curse. Whatever. I can project myself as a spirit to walk the world."

"Astral projection?" I ask, incredulous. "You can seriously do that?"

She nods. "It's not something I can control very well and it really tires me out, but I can find her in spirit form. I just need you to guard my physical body and make sure nothing happens to it while I'm walking in the dreamtime."

"Of course." I nod at her. "Just... how do I know when you're in trouble?"

Alice gives me a wan smile as she pulls her legs up and folds them meditation-style. "I don't know. Maybe I'll start screaming. If that happens?"

She presses a hand to her solar plexus and when it comes away, she's holding a glowing cord of energy in her hand. She gives the cord to me. It burns and tingles and holding it is both exhilarating and uncomfortable.

"If I start screaming, pull me back."

I look down at the energy tether in my hand and I can feel Alice's essence inside it. "Is this part of you?"

"Think of it like a leash," she says. "'Cause I tend to wander."

She takes a deep breath, closes her eyes, and then she's silent.

CHAPTER TWENTY-THREE

RAVYN

I walk through the forest with Broin beside me, happier than I've been since before my family died. I've got friends for the first time, but best of all, I've found someone like Broin in Lockwood. The headmaster is a perfect foil for me and I enjoy him and all of the twisted things he does. I have two men who suit me perfectly.

"You seem awfully pleased with yourself," Broin comments.

"I am. I'm mostly pleased with Lockwood." I smile, squeezing his hand. "It's like I've found another you."

It's meant as a compliment, but he clearly doesn't take it that way. He sets his jaw briefly, then says, "You know you spent the whole night in his office. People will notice." He glances at me and there's both concern and anger in his eyes. "You have to be more discreet."

I sigh. He can be such a buzzkill. "I will. I don't want to get in trouble."

"Good."

He's harshing my buzz, but I think I know where it's coming from. I just wish I understood why he's so worried about something happening to me. He was never this insecure about my safety before. Then again, he never really had any competition, either. He was always able to make sure my playmates were able to look out for me. Little did he know I often had to look out for them, like with Damon.

I decide that I'll let him work this out on his own for a while, considering the rapid changes we've both been through. But if he's still moping and fragile in a week, I'm totally going to call him on it. He needs to trust me like he usually does.

Broin looks up at the sky. "It's the full moon tonight."

I lift my head and smile, basking in the light. "Perfect time for hunting werewolves."

"It's also the perfect time for werewolves to hunt witches," he warns. "They know you survived the attack on the cottage. They're looking for you."

My stomach burns with all the rage and pain I've swallowed since that horrible night. "Then I hope they find me."

"Don't be..."

He's interrupted by the distant howl of a wolf. Its pack calls back and I count seven distinct voices. They're all near the northeast of the woods. I look at Broin and he nods. He shifts into his crow and flies up above the trees to do a little aerial reconnaissance. I pull my dagger and slip through the forest, following the sounds.

They repeat their call and answer and Broin says, —*I see them, many of them, scattered around the forest. If you keep heading in the direction you're going, you'll end up in the middle of the pack.*—

—*Just where I want to be.*—

—*For the love of Lilith, be careful!*—

I creep forward. The woods are alive with whispers tonight and I can feel the weight of a hundred pairs of eyes as I slide through the underbrush. The full moon is a dodgy time to be out and about and when I was younger, Grandma used to keep me and Redera inside until the moon had begun to wane. When I finally got to stand outside in the wind and the light, I felt the power blowing through me and I understood why so many creatures were at their strongest when the moon was full.

As I walk, I hear something in the trees above my head. I'm familiar with the sounds Broin makes when he's following me in his crow form and this is the same sort of thing. Whatever it is that's trailing me is heavier than a crow and I keep my dagger at the ready.

There's a small clearing up ahead. I'm going to have to cross it to get to where those wolves are sending up their third round of call and answer. When I step into the clearing, either my stalker will have to waste time going around, or it'll have to show itself. Either way, it's good for me.

I step into the clearing and almost immediately, a tiny black form appears in front of me. It's bipedal, with bat wings and tiny horns. Sharp fangs overhang its lips and its long, barbed tail swishes as it looks up at me. It's no taller than my knee and if it weren't so ugly-it's-cute, I could kick it into next week. There's no way I'm going to kick this little guy, though.

This is an imp, one of Lucifer's messengers. I guess the Big Guy has something he needs to say.

The imp grins up at me. "Watch your back. You've trusted an enemy."

I open my mouth to ask which enemy, but it vanishes into a puff of smoke. The wolves howl again and Broin tells me, —*They're converging in one spot. There will be too many of them for you to fight at once.*—

—*Then join me.*—

—*Still too many.*—

I only hear seven of them. We can take seven together.

He sounds exasperated. —*Don't assume that all of the wolves are howling. There are more in the forest than you're hearing.*—

—*How many more?*—

--*At least two whole packs are hunting.*— Through our link, I can feel him landing on a branch. He sighs. —*Too dangerous, Little Red.*—

I'm annoyed by this missed opportunity but Broin is right. I can't avenge my family if I get myself killed. That would also send me to Lucifer's clutches early and I don't want that.

Fuck!

I stop and look around, getting my bearings. A flash of white catches my eye and I see Jasper in the bushes, hopping toward me. His eyes are glowing brighter than normal and I see a pale halo of blue around him. Did he follow me? Did Alice send him? Is she the enemy the imp told me about?

I watch the rabbit come closer. Of course Alice isn't the enemy. She's my friend. But Underland is a strange place and they say that betrayal is the name of the game there...

I push those unkind thoughts out of my mind as Jasper hops up to stand at my feet. Alice's breathy little voice speaks. "I found you!"

"Looks like," I whisper.

"You have to come back," she tells me. "It's dangerous. It's the full moon, and the wolves are out."

"I know, but... I have to be out here."

"Why?" she asks, perplexed and concerned. "Does this have to do with your family?"

How does she know about my family?

A wolf howl sounds close by, so close that I actually duck in surprise. Alice gasps and then Jasper disappears. I assume her Sending has been recalled back to Everafter where it belongs.

I'll find out later. I have something else to deal with first.

A twig snaps; I hold perfectly still, crouching amid the bushes. An incautious wolf steps into view, sniffing. Its long teeth are white and glistening in the moonlight, but its blue eyes are dull. I have never seen a wolf with blue eyes.

—Hang tight, Little Red. Don't move.—

The wolf looks around, but somehow it doesn't look at me. It's got its head turned away from me and it's completely vulnerable. It doesn't know I'm here. I slowly rise from my crouch, my dagger in my hand.

I am a witch.

I am here to hunt wolves.

This wolf's luck just ran out.

I launch myself at the wolf, landing on its back. It yelps in surprise and then it screams in pain as I bury my dagger in its neck. I push the blade through and rip and then there's nothing but blood coursing out of its slit throat. The wolf thrashes once, trying to dislodge me and then it drops to the ground.

In death, it transforms back into his human self. He's a middle-aged male, with a nasty set of burn scars on his face. I wonder how he got them, but I'll never know.

—Red!—

—*I'm fine.*—
—*Wait for me.*—

The body at my feet is nude and in life he would have been uninspiring. The only thing of any interest at all is a tattoo on the back of his left shoulder blade. It's the royal seal of Queen Gothel of Grimm City.

Clan She'ol.

My queen.

I can hear more wolves in the vicinity. I had better get away from this bloody mess quickly. The only problem is that at this point, there are more wolves coming closer and I have nowhere to go but up. I clean my dagger and put it back in its sheath, then I climb up into the welcoming arms of a shadow oak.

Broin swoops in and lands on the branch beside me. I point at the tattoo on the corpse below, raising an eyebrow. He shakes his head.

—*Could mean anything.*—

The other wolves burst into the clearing and as soon as they see their fallen comrade, they begin to growl. They sniff the ground around them furiously and I know that it's just a matter of time before they realize where I've gone. Broin watches them closely, his tension amplifying mine.

This is trouble.

There are three wolves here. One of them is clearly the leader and he whines at the dead body. I guess he just lost someone he cared about. *Sucks to be you, fuckhead.*

Now they'll know what it feels like to have your loved ones slain for no reason.

They shift into their human forms. The leader is standing with his back to me so I can't see his face. He speaks softly to the others and they gather up their fallen friend. One of them is wearing an amulet around his neck, the kind that magic users pack with spells and sell to the mundane. He activates the spell and he, one of his buddies and the corpse all translocate. The leader sighs and shifts back into wolf form. I try to get a better look at him, but it's too dark up in the tree.

The wolves in the forest howl and he howls back. He scratches at the dirt, tossing leaves and grass over the bloodstain my kill left behind. I want to jump on him and kill him, too, but Broin is giving me a pointed look.

—*Enough adventures for tonight,*— he says.

—*You're getting in my way,*— I snap. —*Stop trying to protect me.*—

—*Never.*—

The wolf trots out of the clearing toward the howling and I lose my chance to add another ornamental stitch to my cloak, like notches in a scoreboard. At least I get to put one on from tonight.

We wait until the sound of the wolf vanishes completely. Broin, whose hearing as a crow is more sensitive than even my augmented senses, listens closely. Finally, he nods.

—*Let's go.*—

He drops down to the ground and resumes his man shape. I jump down too and he catches me in his strong arms before my boots can hit the ground. Our eyes meet and he puts me gently on my feet.

"Well done, Little Red," he whispers. "You've earned a reward."

I grin. Too bad there are too many wolves around right now for me to collect the reward. I grab his hand and we head back toward Everafter.

Chapter Twenty-Four

Lockwood

It's my duty as headmaster to secure Everafter when the moon is full. I've been informed by the staff that all of the students are accounted for and it's safe to close the gates and set the locks. The locks are accessed from the inside of most of the gates, but the main one requires a key to lock it from the outside. That leaves me outside the gates as the moon rises higher in the sky.

How convenient.

I'm the Alpha of my pack, which pleases neither me nor the wolves I command. I've left my younger brother in charge of things while I'm here at Everafter and so far, this arrangement has suited me.

No longer.

Ravyn has re-awakened something rooted deep within me, a darkness that I've tried to expunge. She is reminding me of the pleasures of control, of domination, of having someone completely at my mercy. She's changed me and it remains to be seen whether that change is for good or for ill.

The pack will learn what it means to be controlled and they will learn to toe the line I draw for them. For too long they've been unruly and lawless, following only their own desires and sporadic whims. Their king, my brother, has allowed it and they've gained the worst reputation of all of the packs in She'ol. No - they've more than gained it. They've earned it. Their brutality, something I once revelled in as well, is becoming infamous. Even packs far from Grimm City have heard of us and when we enter their lands, they're rightfully afraid.

We hunt relentlessly.

We kill without conscience.

We are Witch Hunters.

The moonlight caresses me and I feel my blood rising to answer it. I hear my pack howling to me and it's time to remind them who their alpha really is. I shift into my wolf form and howl back. My voice is loud and they respond immediately, calling me to join them.

I'm a new wolf and they will learn to obey me.

Or else.

To Be Continued...

THANK YOU

Thank you for reading **Once Upon A Wolf**. Your support is extremely valued! If you enjoyed this book, **please consider leaving a review on Amazon**. It's really important for us as self-publishing authors, who don't have the backing of an established press. Not to mention we love to hear from our readers!

YOU MIGHT ALSO ENJOY...

GRIM: DEATH'S APPRENTICE BOOK 1
URBAN FANTASY REVERSE HAREM

Https: www.amazon.com/ebook/dp/B07QYRLHVN

YOU MIGHT ALSO ENJOY...

What could be worse than getting hit by a bus? Waking up as Death's new apprentice, that's what.

I already know how crazy that sounds.

For 18 years, I was able to see the dead, so I pretty much managed to deal with a lot of unusual things in the world. I even learned to accept my strange, if not slightly annoying, "I see dead people" ability. But the one thing that tipped me over the edge? I can't drink coffee in the afterlife.

Not even a sip.

I know what you're thinking. Surely things can't get any worse than *that?* Well... I also have a rival apprentice who despises me, a quarterback ghost who won't leave me the hell alone, a sexy angel determined to take me out on a date, and a silly little crush on my new boss.

Yeah, you read that last part right. I have an aimless crush on the Grim Reaper, and no, he isn't a hooded skeleton clutching a scythe. He's a gorgeous man in a tailor-made suit and every word he utters fills me with desire...just like the others do, despite my best efforts to resist them.

Unfortunately, a pack of demons are now interfering with the human world, and Death has tasked me with putting an end to them. At least, that's what I tell myself, as I quite possibly make the worst decisions of my entire life...

Death's Apprentice is a Reverse Harem Urban Fantasy. This series is a slow-burn romance filled

with an extreme amount of dark humor, sarcasm, mystery, and a talking dog who is totally judging Sacha's bad decisions in life. Buckle up, and get ready to join Sacha on her soul-reaping journey...and perhaps a little detour into Hell.

APPENDIX ONE: CHARACTERS

STUDENTS and THEIR FAMILIARS:

Ravyn Hemlock, Clan She'ol, Mandrake Coven
Redera Hemlock, Ravyn's twin
Elnora Hemlock, Ravyn's grandmother
Maxim Hemlock, Ravyn's grandfather
Esmeralda Hemlock, Ravyn's three-times great-grandmother
Broin Blackstone, former druid, now witch and crow shapeshifter - Ravyn's Daddy
Mephisto, Ravyn's horse
Alice Underland
Jasper, a rabbit, Alice's familiar
Princess Sirena of Poseida
Augustus, a crab, Sirena's familiar
Prince Erik of Aira
Princess Aurora of Talia
Princess Cinder of Wysteria
Princess Rapunzel of Fantasia
Prince Christopher of Fantasia

APPENDIX ONE: CHARACTERS

Prince Gideon
Fang, a wolf-dog, Gideon's familiar
Hansel
Gretl
Marcin

EVERAFTER ACADEMY FACULTY AND STAFF:

Headmaster Dane Lockwood
Professor Nightingale, Magical Studies
Professor Clarinda Rumpkin, Potions
Professor Martha Huckleberry, Enchantments
Professor Abdiel, Familiar Handling
Professor Hua Mulan, Defence
Mrs. Philomena Thornton, Head of the First Year Students
Mrs. Beauty, librarian
Quasidmodo, the groundskeeper
Aladdin, Quasimodo's assistant

POLITICAL BODIES:

Maleficis Invictus, the Witches' High Coven
Covenmaster: Reverend Cassim Salvador
The High Council, Leaders of the Western Wood
The Falcon Knights, a knightly order in Fantasia

GODS:

The Storyteller
Lucfier (Satan, the Fallen One, the Prince of Lies, the Morningstar)

APPENDIX TWO: KINGDOMS

The Eastern Wood:

<u>DROAICH</u>
Capital: Grimm City
Rulers: Queen Gothel
King Bane

The Western Wood:

<u>POSEIDA</u>
Capital: Delphina
Rulers: King Merkin
Princess Hagera
Princess Sirena

<u>FANTASIA</u>
Capital: Reyna
Rulers: Queen Laurette
Prince Christopher
Princess Rapunzel

APPENDIX TWO: KINGDOMS

AIRA
Capital: Zephyr
Rulers: King Gareth
Queen Isabelle
Prince Erik
Prince Tristan

WYSTERIA
Capital: Ember City
Rulers: Regent, Lord Adair
Princess Cinder

TALIA
Capital: The Citadel
Rulers: Queen Rosalie
King Stefan
Princess Aurora

APPENDIX THREE: WITCH COVENS

Mandrake Coven
Nightshade Coven
Ricinus Coven
Oleander Coven
Cassava Coven
Botuli Coven

APPENDIX FOUR: WOLF PACKS

Russo Lupa Pack - Witch Hunters
Penny Royal Pack - Witch Hunters

ABOUT TIEGAN

Tiegan Clyne has been writing for longer than most of her friends have been alive. She loves music, dark fantasy, and telling stories. Tiegan is a crazy cat lady in training and an all-around good egg. You can follow her here:

Facebook:
https://www.facebook.com/tiegan.clyne.37

Facebook Reader's Group:
https://www.facebook.com/groups/654177788313017

OTHER BOOKS BY TIEGAN

Amazon: https://www.amazon.com/Tiegan-Clyne/e/B07PWYS4W5

ABOUT SCARLETT

Scarlett Snow comes from a big family in a small Scottish town and has always strived to prove that if you are passionate about something, no one can stop you from chasing your dreams. She lives with her wolf dog and kitties and is unashamedly addicted to coffee.

If you'd like to join her newsletter to be kept updated on her books, you can do so here:

www.scarlett.katzesnow.com

Facebook Page:
   https://www.facebook.com/authorscarlettsnow/

Facebook Reader's Group:
   https://www.facebook.com/groups/scarlettscoven

OTHER BOOKS BY SCARLETT

Amazon: https://www.amazon.com/Scarlett-Snow/e/B07NKFPSKN

Non-Amazon Book: https://payhip.com/b/K8Mr

Scarlett also writes under Katze Snow (Dark M/M Books): https://www.amazon.com/Katze-Snow/e/B01M0GTAED

Printed in Poland
by Amazon Fulfillment
Poland Sp. z o.o., Wrocław